MICAH'S GOT TALENT?

ALSO AVAILABLE:

THE BIG FAIL

COMING SOON:

TO SKETCH A THIEF

JUST CHILL

Micah was supposed to be reading. And not just because, as a general rule of life, reading is better than thinking about video games. No, he was supposed to be reading because he was sitting in class with his teacher telling him to read. So, yeah. He should probably start reading.

But first, his eyes rolled across the brightly colored alphabet on the wall in front of him. Mrs. Grittner was nice enough, but she was new to the fifth grade.

the kid who everybody knows is going to be famous someday.

Sorry, still not Micah.

Micah is just another kid in the crowd. He'll occasionally rise to the lofty heights of "average," but more often settles for "good enough" or "at least I'm not the worst." There is nothing particularly special about him, nothing to make him stand out or get noticed. Which is fine with him. He isn't a big fan of being the center of attention anyway.

Who needs to be special when there are video games to play?

Captain Karate Dino Cop 3 is his favorite game. But he already beat it. Micah has been racking his brain all morning for a way to convince his parents to upgrade his system to the Ultra Game-A-Tron 64. His current gaming system is so old it can't play the new version: *Captain Karate Dino Cop 4*. Plus, the commercial says the graphics are . . .

"64x better!"

ULTRA GAME-A-TRON 64

You probably also know that kid who is the best at every sport without even trying. They're the quarterbacks who throw a touchdown on every play. The first time they ever faced a curveball, they knocked it over the fence. They're an eagle flying among turkeys, a thoroughbred in a herd of donkeys, a rabbit in a tortoise race. (And not the ridiculous kind of rabbit that stops to nap halfway through the race!) They're the one who always gets picked first, and their team wins every time.

Nope, Micah isn't that kid either.

And then there's the kid who is truly an artist in every sense of the word. They create museum-worthy masterpieces with Crayola markers, or write poetry that would bring tears to the eyes of the most hardened gym teacher. They can wow a crowd with their violin at age six, then switch to bassoon at age nine and perform with the Boston Symphony Orchestra. Their fourth grade essay, "What I Did over Summer Break" is called "An absolute triumph!" by the *New York Times*. They're

CHAPTER ONE

You know how every school has a kid who's so smart it's a little scary? They seem to know everything about everything, from the most poisonous snake in Asia, to the capital of Vanuatu, to the name of the vice president's pet iguana. And they read everything they can get their hands on, not just books, but cereal boxes, Chinese take-out menus—even T-shirt tags! They can do ridiculously hard math problems with fractions and decimals and square roots (whatever those are)—and they don't even use their fingers!

You know the kid I'm talking about.

Micah Murphy is *not* that kid.

Copyright © 2019 by Hachette Book Group
Published in association with JellyTelly Press

Cover copyright © 2019 by Hachette Book Group

FaithWords is a division of Hachette Book Group, Inc. The FaithWords name and logo are trademarks of Hachette Book Group, Inc.

JellyTelly Press is a division of Winsome Truth, Inc.

FaithWords
Hachette Book Group
1290 Avenue of the Americas, New York, NY 10104

hachettebookgroup.com | faithwords.com | jellytelly.com

Micah's Super Vlog trademark and character rights are owned by Square One World Media, Inc., and used by permission. Micah's Super Vlog was created by Girish Manuel for Square One World Media, Inc.

Written by Andy McGuire
Illustrated by Girish Manuel
Layout by Sarah Siegand

First Edition: June 2019

Library of Congress Cataloging-in-Publication Data has been applied for.

ISBN: 978-1-5460-2661-7 (trade paperback), 978-1-5460-3353-0 (hardcover), 978-1-5460-2660-0 (ebook)

Printed in the USA.
LSC-C
10 9 8 7 6 5 4 3 2 1

MICAH'S GOT TALENT?

BY ANDY MCGUIRE

ILLUSTRATIONS BY GIRISH MANUEL

Embarrassing Stuff in Miss Grittner's Fifth-Grade Classroom

- Alphabet banner over the whiteboard, with pictures of blocks and xylophones

- Safety scissors barely sharp enough to cut through a slice of American cheese

- Giant Lego blocks with eyes on them for making cute animals, like ducks and ponies

- Play-Doh (actually, I'm okay with this one since it's the spaghetti factory set—an absolute classic)

- Two posters of a certain smiling, purple dinosaur

- Half-eaten sticks of glue

She used to be a kindergarten teacher and still decorated like one. Micah suspected if he looked hard enough he'd find big fat pencils and finger paints somewhere in the room. Ah, kindergarten. A simpler time.

Finally, he let his eyes wander back across the page. It was actually a pretty good book. It was science fiction, his favorite.

The book was about a three-headed alien who always seemed to be arguing. With himself. The three heads were named Zargon, Blarnok, and Steve. Zargon and Blarnok didn't care for Steve. He was no good at alien games and always complained about being chilly. That's a hard problem to solve when you share a body.

"Do you get the point of this story?" Micah whispered to his friend Lydia, sitting next to him.

Lydia was smart. Like knows-the-capital-of-Vanuatu-smart. But unlike some brainiac kids, she was also kind enough to help Micah when he was in a pinch. She nodded. "I think it's about learning how to get along with others. Or it could be about learning how to appreciate someone who's different from you. This is only the first chapter, so we still need to see where it goes."

"Huh," said Micah. "I thought maybe it was about a regular person who's just dreaming he's a three-headed alien."

Lydia rolled her eyes. "You think every story is just a dream."

Micah had to admit this was true, ever since *The Wizard of Oz* blew his mind in the third grade.

It was almost time for lunch. Mrs. Grittner turned on the TV so the class could watch *The PB and J Report*. PB and J were the school's celebrity news correspondents, so if you wanted the straight scoop about who's who and what's what, you paid attention. It was hard not to. Every sentence they'd ever spoken ended with an exclamation mark!

Suddenly, PB's voice silenced Micah's thoughts. "Breaking news! Four weeks from today, New Leaf Elementary School will host our fifth annual Talent Extravaganza! This year's show is guaranteed to be the biggest talent show in the school's history!"

"The biggest talent show in ANY school's history!" said J.

"Any student can enter, and the winner receives an Ultra Game-A-Tron 64!"

Micah sat up straight and started really listening now.

"It will be the event of the year!" said PB. "All students are welcome to show off their talents to the whole school!"

J piped in. "Singing, dancing, magic, juggling, you name it!"

"I hope there's a mime!" said PB. "I love mimes!"

"Mimes? Really?" J looked at PB and raised an eyebrow. "If you say so."

PB ignored her. "Everybody mark your calendars for four weeks from today. The gym will be packed with students, parents, teachers, and maybe even the local news!"

"I heard Channel 7 might come! Stormy McAllister is the best!"

"Nobody announces snow days like Stormy!"

"Well, there you have it! The talent show will be the event of the year!"

"If you want to be a part of the show, just sign your name on the sheet outside the lunchroom!"

"It'll be sensational!"

"See you there!"

The bell for lunch rang, and everyone got up to go. All Micah could think about was winning that Ultra Game-A-Tron 64. It was the best device out there, and it was going to be his! It was two whole versions newer than the system he had now, which meant he'd finally be able to get *Captain Karate Dino Cop 4*!

He walked right up to the sign-up sheet, grabbed a marker from his backpack, and signed his name in big, bold letters. He was marking his territory, and no one could stop him!

He couldn't wait to stand up in front of everyone in the gym and . . .

And what, exactly?

Did he play an instrument? No. Sing? No. Dance? No. Juggle? Not that he was aware of.

A cold sweat washed over him. With a rush of horror, he screamed in his head, *WHAT HAVE I DONE?!?*

Got Talent?

How can a simple signature ruin my entire year? I should have used a pencil, but NO, I'm such a genius, I signed up for the talent show with INK! Now, my fate is sealed, and the whole school will see that I'm boring and completely UNtalented.

I know God created me special. I just thought He'd have clued me in by now about what exactly makes me special.

I could beg my way out of this (enough to make Miss Petunia abandon her goal of getting every student up onstage before they leave New Leaf Elementary School). But I want that Ultra Game-A-Tron 64 more than I want to save myself from mind-blowing embarrassment. So, I guess the next four weeks are going to be spent finding something I'm even a little good at. This should lead to epic failure . . . er, I mean . . . fun.

I praise you, for I am fearfully and wonderfully made. Wonderful are your works; my soul knows it very well. Psalm 139:14 (ESV)

 What talents do YOU think Micah should try?

 What talents do YOU have? (Micah needs all the ideas he can get!)

CHAPTER TWO

Micah stared at the tater tots on his plate. They seemed to stare right back at him, questioning his life choices. He couldn't blame them.

What had he been thinking? Who signs up for a talent show when you don't even have a talent . . . to show?

Everyone in the lunchroom seemed excited but him. He looked around at the tables filled with chatty fifth graders who no longer had to use their "classroom voices." Even the walls were enthusiastic, covered with inspirational posters that said stuff like "Reach for the stars!" or "You can go anywhere your imagination takes you!" Right now, he imagined a hole in the ground, where he could hide from his troubles. That probably wasn't what the wall had in mind.

A part of him hoped nobody would sit with him, just so he could think about his problem in peace. On the other hand, he didn't want to be the kid who eats by himself.

Luckily, there was no need to worry about that. Micah watched his friends Armin and Gabe pay for their lunches and walk over to his table. "What's up, Micah?" Gabe asked.

"What's up is I'm an idiot. I just did the dumbest thing I've ever done."

"That's saying something," said Armin. "What did you do?"

"I signed up for the talent show."

Lydia walked over from the lunch line and put her tray down. "But I didn't know you had any talents, Micah."

"I don't."

"That's not true," Armin said. "Didn't I see you pull a rabbit out of your hat once?"

"No, that was just a sock that stuck to my hat in the dryer."

"That's even better!" said Gabe. "I love socks."

Lydia ignored Gabe's comment. "If you don't have a talent, then why did you sign up?"

"Because the winner gets a new Ultra Game-A-Tron 64. I've wanted one forever, and my parents refuse to spend that kind of money. So, when I saw the sign-up sheet, I figured I was destined to win the talent show."

"Do you now see the flaw in your plan?" Lydia asked.

"You mean the fact that I don't have a talent?"

"That's the one."

"Then yes."

Mr. Turtell paced back and forth near their table. He had lunch duty that week, and he liked to keep a careful watch to make sure no one added salt to their tots. Such frivolous behavior is irresponsible.

It would surely lead to overexcited fifth graders, and there was nothing worse to Mr. Turtell than excitement. When it came to food, Mr. Turtell used the word "bland" as a compliment.

"Micah, I hear you have a dilemma," Mr. Turtell said.

Micah looked up, surprised that Mr. Turtell would get involved. "Do you think you could get me out of the talent show?"

"While I'm generally opposed to entertainment of any sort on school grounds, I would never dream of undermining the authority of a sign-up sheet."

Micah stared up at him, not exactly sure what was happening.

Mr. Turtell went on. "But I may be able to help."

"I'd love any help I can get."

"Well then, let me list all the talents you don't have. That way we can narrow things down. You don't juggle, you don't do magic tricks, you don't whistle, you don't dance . . ."

"Actually," Armin said, "it might be easier if we

divide up what you don't do into categories. For instance, we could start with the musical instruments you don't play. You don't play guitar or piano or violin or saxophone . . ."

"Or sitar or lyre or pan flute," added Lydia.

"But you've never *tried* to learn the pan flute, Micah," Gabe said. "You can do it! I believe in you!" he trilled.

"Thanks," said Micah. "But I don't know if this is the best way for me to figure out what my talent is. Anyway, it's time to go to recess."

As the four friends got up to go, they could still hear Mr. Turtell mumbling in the background. "Or breathe fire or ride a unicycle or train tigers or make a quiche or . . ."

The sky was blue, and the sun was shining brightly outside, mocking Micah's foul mood. He and his friends walked across the pavement to get to the triangle of mulch between the playground and the ball fields. They rarely hung out on the playground, because it was the elementary-school version of rush hour, filled with crashes, stop-and-go traffic, and cops (er . . . teachers). Meanwhile, the ball fields were teeming with the school's superstar athletes playing soccer or football and arguing over every play like it was the Super Bowl.

But the mulchy space between, what Micah and his friends called no-man's-land, was a peaceful oasis where you could sit and talk or play a friendly game of giant Jenga.

"Lydia, did you sign up for the talent show?" Micah asked.

"Yeah. I think I'm going to play a Schubert piece on the piano."

Gabe squinched up his face. "Play with a piece of sherbet on a piano?"

"Schubert. He's a composer."

"Do you even care about winning the prize?" Armin asked. "I didn't think you liked video games."

"I don't. If I win, I'll probably just sell it and buy books."

Micah sighed. He turned to Armin. "What are you going to do for the talent show?"

"I can't decide between a hacky sack trick I've been working on or a juggling routine. Either way, if I win, I'm keeping the Ultra Game-A-Tron 64!"

Micah shrugged. "You both have a much better chance than me. You can do everything! I can't do anything."

"That's ridiculous," Lydia said. "No one can do everything."

"Except maybe Frank Millwood," Armin said.

Frank Millwood was the best athlete in fifth grade, but he also got good grades, played the drums, and even knew how to use shading to make his superhero drawings look 3-D. But what made him even more annoying was the fact that he was a nice guy, so everyone liked him. Ugh!

Lydia shook her head. "I'm sure even Frank Millwood can't do *everything*. Don't worry about him. Comparing yourself to others will drive you crazy."

Micah sat down in the mulch, not even caring if he got the back of his pants dirty. He might as well build up a tolerance for kids making fun of him.

On his way toward the mulch triangle, Armin had grabbed a soccer ball from the ball bin. He dropped it onto his left foot, kicked it back and forth several times, then flipped it up to catch it again.

"I'm sure you could do something simple like that," Armin said, handing Micah the ball and pulling him to his feet.

Micah got two kicks, tripped over his own leg, and fell back down on the mulch.

"Maybe you could yo-yo," said Gabe. "I bet you could do some easy tricks." He took a yo-yo out of his pocket and quickly made it sleep, did a perfect "walk the dog," then flipped it into an "around the world." Micah had never tried to yo-yo before, but there was no way Gabe was more talented than he was!

Gabe unlooped the string of the yo-yo from his

finger and handed it over. Micah put his middle finger in the loop, released it to the ground, and then tried to yank it back up again. The yo-yo completely ignored him and rolled away until it ran out of string. It lay there on the ground, mocking him, just like the tater tots and the sunshine.

"Well . . . ," said Lydia, clearly struggling to think of anything to suggest, "I'm sure you can whistle, right?"

Micah puckered up and blew a thin stream of air through his lips. Nothing. Not even a half-hearted teapot sound.

They sat silently as fifth graders shrieked and screamed all around them, playing games of freeze tag and four square. Recess wasn't an ideal spot for figuring things out, but apparently, nothing could stop Lydia's brain when she had a problem to solve. Micah could tell from the look on her face that something brilliant was about to pop out of her mouth.

"Maybe Gabe was right!" she said.

"He was?" Armin asked.

"I was?" Gabe repeated. No one was more surprised at Gabe being right than Gabe.

Micah looked at Lydia questioningly. "You mean about me playing the pan flute?"

"Kind of. Well . . . not exactly. What Gabe actually said was that you've never tried it. That's the secret. You just have to try as many things as possible. You'll find your talent; I'm sure of it!"

"The talent show is four weeks away," Armin said.

Lydia nodded. "Yeah, that's plenty of time."

"Is it?" Micah asked. "It feels impossible."

Gabe slapped him on the back. "You can do it!"

The end-of-recess bell rang, and kids stampeded toward the doors.

As they followed the crowd, Micah was still thinking about the task ahead of him. "But I'm just not good at anything. You all found your talents right away."

"That's not true," said Armin. "I tried several sports before soccer. Sometimes you have to experiment with a bunch of things before something clicks."

"I tried drums before I figured out I was better at piano and violin," Lydia said. "When I first started playing the drums, my brother said it sounded like a car crashing into the side of a building. Then I tried the piano, and it all came together."

"We'll help you figure it out," said Armin. "I can try to teach you to juggle, and Lydia can try to teach you an easy song on the piano."

"And I can teach you to yo-yo," Gabe added. He pulled the yo-yo out of his pocket, did an "around the world," and accidentally whacked Lydia on the side of the cheek.

"Or maybe you could learn to yo-yo from YouTube," said Lydia, rubbing her face.

"Just remember," Armin said, "we only have to find *one* thing you're good at. So, don't get discouraged if you strike out a few times. Like we said, no one's good at everything."

As they waited in line to go back into the building, they could see Frank heading in from the far end of the soccer field.

"Is he doing what I think he's doing?" Armin asked in an awed whisper.

"Yes, I think he is," Lydia whispered back.

Frank jogged to the back of the line while dribbling a soccer ball on one foot, yo-yoing up and down, and whistling the latest Dreem Doodz hit.

"Well," said Lydia, "*Almost* no one's good at everything."

Gabe shook his head. "I bet he can't pull a sock out of his hat."

But Micah wasn't listening to Gabe's attempt at encouragement. He just glared at annoying

Frank Millwood. *What would it be like to be good at everything?* he thought to himself. Right now, he'd settle for being good at *anything*.

Thank God I Have Friends

If I don't find my talent soon, I'll be standing onstage in a few weeks like a total idiot. I'll be laughed at . . . No one will want to be my friend . . . Girls will never talk to me! I won't ever get a job, and then I'll be homeless! I cannot let that happen!

At least for now, Armin, Gabe, and Lydia are helping me. And on the bright side, if Armin wins, which—let's face it—is much more likely than *me* winning, he'll definitely invite me over for some awesome *Captain Karate Dino Cop* action!

I'm so thankful for the friends God has given me. I could not survive this torture without them. They've been so great! I'd like to think it's because I'm a good friend too. I can't believe I'm going to admit this, but I'm starting to think friendship is more important than video games. Too bad being a good friend isn't considered a talent.

A friend loves at all times.
Proverbs 17:17 (ESV)

▷ **Would YOU laugh at the kid who gets up onstage and makes a fool of himself?**

▷ **How do YOU say thanks to your friends? (Micah would love to do something nice for Armin, Gabe, and Lydia!)**

CHAPTER THREE

On Micah's walk home from school that day, the sky was a perfect blue, flowers scented the air, and robins and bluebirds sang their adorable hearts out. It was all terrible. To Micah, the sky was the color of moldy cheese, the air smelled like his dad's lawn mowing shoes, and the birds sounded like his sister yelling at him to get out of her room. The world shouldn't pretend to be a beautiful place when Micah knew better.

Micah's house was smallish, squarish, and bluish with white trim. The garage door was already open when he got there, which meant at least one parent was home. He wasn't sure he was ready to tell either of them about his day, so Micah went around to the back of his house, so he didn't have to talk to anyone. Only his dog, Barnabas, greeted him. Just like he'd hoped. Barnabas was a small, scrawny mutt who didn't ask any questions.

Micah trudged through the list of things he always had to finish before he could have any screen time. First, he did his chores: taking out the garbage, picking up his room, and feeding Skippy, his box turtle. Then he got to work on his math and spelling homework, trying to ignore the worries stirring in his belly as he focused on multiplying fractions and making sure he used enough *r*s in the word *embarrass*. (Why on earth did it need two of them?) At last, his mom called him out of his room for dinner.

Now he had a decision to make. He could keep his troubles to himself, so he didn't have to talk about what an idiot he was, or he could share the burden with his mom, dad, and sister. Two of the three of them would be supportive, and the other one already thought he was an idiot, so no loss there.

They sat down to a delicious meal of baked ham with pineapple slices. It was like sawdust in his mouth.

"Micah, you've been awfully quiet since you got home," his dad said. "How was your day?"

Micah jumped right in. "Not great. There's a talent show in four weeks, and the whole school is coming to watch. Even parents are invited. And the winner gets an Ultra Game-A-Tron 64!"

"That sounds like fun!" said his mom.

"And I signed up for it."

"Even better," said his dad.

"Not better at all!" said Micah. "I don't have a talent."

"Ha!" said Micah's sister, Audrey, in a tone that said this was really more of a sarcastic exclamation than a laugh. "You can say that again."

"Oh, Micah," sighed his mom. "That's not true. You have plenty of talents!"

"Like?" asked Micah.

"Like?" echoed Audrey.

"Like that time you played 'Twinkle, Twinkle, Little Star' for your preschool graduation with all your little friends."

"You played a mean triangle!" said his dad.

His mom went on. "Let's see . . . Ben played the kazoo. Armin was on the wood block. And Lydia! She played a top-notch xylophone!"

His dad held up his corn to the side of his head with a goofy grin on his face. "It was music to my ears."

Everyone just stared at him.

"Get it? An ear of corn? Music to my ears?"

His mom patted his dad on the hand and looked back at Micah. "We both thought you were great, honey."

Micah knew they were just trying to be helpful, but inside he felt a little exasperated. "Mom, that performance was six years ago!"

"And it sounded like someone stepped on a cat," said Audrey.

"You could be kinder to your brother," said his father to Audrey.

"Maybe so," she answered. "But believe me: it would not be kind to anyone if we encouraged him to get the old band back together."

He could always count on Audrey for honesty. Support and comfort, not so much. But sometimes he needed someone to tell him the flat-out truth. If he wanted to build his confidence before he had to give a speech in class, he'd absolutely go to Mom or Dad. But if he needed someone to tell him his parrot shirt did NOT work with his orange cargo shorts or teach him a hard lesson about how he should never admit that he still watched *Wonder Pets*—she was his girl.

"I've just got to win that Ultra Game-A-Tron 64. It's my only hope of getting one before another version comes out!" Micah gave his parents a disappointed look. They weren't falling for it.

"Well, there have to be other talents you could show off," Micah's mom encouraged.

"You're always doing tricks with Barnabas," said his dad. "The other day, didn't I see you two synchronized swimming together? You looked so graceful!"

"I was just fishing Nerf bullets out of the pool. For some reason, Barnabas jumped in after me."

"Either way, it was breathtaking!" said his mom.

"Breathtakingly ridiculous," mumbled Audrey.

"Maybe it's something to build on," suggested his dad.

Who Should I Ask?

When I'm in a jam and just need some encouraging words, it's best to go to my mom and dad. But when I need honest feedback, my sister is the one to talk to.

Who do YOU think I should ask for advice in these situations?

DAD AUDREY MOM

- Do these beet and pumpernickel brownies I baked taste okay?
- Do you think I should give some of them to Mr. Beaker before I take my science test?
- Should I add the *Wonder Pets* theme song to the playlist for my fifth-grade birthday party?
- Do you think everyone had fun at my fifth-grade birthday party?
- Should I get a haircut before my school pictures?
- Does my new haircut make me look like a giant mushroom?

Micah was glad for the encouragement but didn't feel a whole lot closer to figuring out what he should do for the show. "Don't worry," he said with a sigh. "I'll think of something."

After he and Audrey cleaned up the dinner dishes, Micah grabbed a handful of berries for dessert and went outside on his front porch to think. Barnabas looked up at him, drool dripping from his jowls. Micah tossed a berry up in the air, and Barnabas caught it easily in his mouth.

"Good job, boy," said Micah.

This gave Micah an idea for the talent show. He tossed a second berry in the air, higher this time, so he could catch it himself.

Clunk. It landed on his forehead and stuck there.

Micah shook his head and looked at Barnabas staring up at him. "I guess even *you* are more talented than I am."

He scratched the dog behind his ears and thought some more. But maybe there was still something to his dad's dog tricks idea. It certainly wasn't the worst suggestion he'd heard that day.

Micah looked through an old toy bin in the garage and found a purple hula hoop with silver glitter. If his idea worked, he'd have to paint the hoop before the show. It wouldn't be smart for a fifth-grade boy to feature glitter in his act.

He walked the hoop back over to the porch and held it against the ground beside Barnabas. The dog lay flat against the cool, shaded stone, with only his eyes following Micah and the hoop. The rest of him might as well have been a lawn ornament.

"Barnabas, jump!" Micah commanded.

Barnabas's ears twitched up. Nothing else budged.

"Barnabas! Jump!" Micah spoke louder and more forcefully.

Nothing.

"Barnabas! Go through the hoop!"

This time his ears didn't even quiver.

Micah tried another way. He lifted Barnabas's

head and front paws and put them in the hoop. "Through the hoop, Barnabas!"

Barnabas sat up, with half of him now sticking out of each side of the hoop. A small part of the hoop, meanwhile, was glistening with dog spit.

"Vat do you zink you're doing?"

Micah had been so focused on the feats of Barnabas the Amazing that he'd failed to notice Hanz walking up the sidewalk. Hanz was the richest, most obnoxious kid in school. His family had come over from Germany because his dad was the president of a technology company with a new research lab in Micah's town.

Hanz was so rich and had so much cool technology, it was like he lived in the future. His world was filled with robot butlers, hovercrafts, and life-sized *Star Wars* spaceships. If he wanted it, he'd get it—even if it hadn't been invented yet.

"Trying to teach my dog a trick," said Micah.

"Zat's supposed to be a dog? I zought it vas a dead possum you'd found in ze road. Smells like roadkill to me, but I guess I'll take your vord for it."

Micah was used to insults from Hanz. He was getting better at shrugging them off, but for some reason, it hit harder when his dog was involved. "What do *you* know? You think you're any better at teaching a dog tricks?"

As soon as he said it, Micah knew it was a mistake. Hanz had been waiting for the chance to remind him how much better he was at everything. Yet again. "My robot dog, Pouncer, is ze most brilliant dog on ze planet. He can read Braille and make roast beef sandviches. He uses ze toilet like a person, lifting ze seat and flushing every time. He never misses ze bowl. I'm teaching him how to fly my hovercraft, and NASA has been begging me to put him in zeir new space program for gifted robot dogs."

"I don't believe any of it," said Micah. Actually, he believed every word of it. He'd seen enough marvels from Hanz to know he was probably telling the truth.

"Believe vatever you vant," said Hanz. "But you'll see ze truth when my robot dog does tricks in ze talent show." He laughed his haughty laugh and started to walk away. In the distance, Micah could hear Hanz talking to himself. "Ha! Even my robot turtle Vladimir could jump zrough a silly hula hoop!"

Hanz reached into his pocket and pulled out what looked like a cell phone. He threw it at the ground, and in an instant, it unfolded into a hoverboard. Hanz jumped on top of it and waved at Micah as he slowly zoomed away.

"Just let me know if you vant zat dead possum turned into a hat. I know a guy."

Micah gave up and went inside. The worry in his stomach was just getting worse, and he was having trouble feeling any glimmers of hope.

The phone rang, and Micah answered. (Yup, Micah's family still has a landline. So old-school!)

"Hello."

"Hey Micah. It's Armin. My mom said you could

come over this weekend so we could figure out your talent. Maybe we'll try something with a basketball?"

"Thanks, Armin! I'll ask my mom and dad."

"Great. See you tomorrow at school."

Well, even if he was going to humiliate himself in front of the whole school, at least he still had a few good friends who would stick by him.

Ugh! Hanz!

Hanz always seems to show up at the worst times . . . bragging about all the cool stuff he has. A robot dog? I mean . . . yeah, sure, that's pretty cool, but . . . does he have to be so cruel? How could someone who has so much be so mean?! I don't know why I let him get to me.

My parents sure are trying to be encouraging. They just want me to win that Ultra Game-A-Tron 64 so they don't have to buy me one. It would be great to win it. I just don't see how that's going to happen. I'm sure Hanz would agree.

Whatever. I can't let Hanz get under my skin. I need to focus on finding a talent or getting out of this show. I remember my parents telling me that one of the best ways to protect yourself from hurtful people is to pray for them. At first, it sounded crazy, but I'm starting to wonder if maybe they were right.

Love your enemies!
Pray for those who persecute you!
Matthew 5:44 (NLT)

 How do YOU handle mean kids and bullies at your school?

 What should Micah do when someone says something mean to him?

CHAPTER FOUR

Day: Friday

Time Until the Talent Show: 3 weeks, 6 days, 8 hours, and 15 minutes

What's Happening at School Today: Art class (AKA epic embarrassment displayed on an easel)

At 10:15 a.m. every day, Mrs. Grittner's fifth graders went to a different specialty class: gym on Monday, science lab on Tuesday, technology on Wednesday, music on Thursday, and art on Friday. Micah neither loved nor hated art. He didn't spend much time thinking about art at all. He just knew he wasn't particularly good at it.

As usual, the classroom smelled like acrylic paints and sweaty children. It was decorated with posters of art loved by elementary-school kids across the country: a Monet water lily, Picasso's blue guitar player, two M. C. Escher optical illusions, and a classic—a vintage Mickey Mouse.

"Today you can keep working on your soul search paintings," Mr. Spinoza instructed, once the students were all seated at their easels.

It was day two of Spinoza's famous "soul search assignment." Most fifth graders seemed to love it, but it was a little too unstructured for Micah's taste. Mr. Spinoza wanted them to search inside their inner beings and paint what they most wanted deep in their hearts. Fame? Money? World peace? Longer recess? But they couldn't just paint the thing itself, they had to paint a picture that *represented* the thing. Micah would have rather just painted a bowl of fruit or a couple of Hot Wheels cars, like they did in fourth grade.

"I totally get what you're doing there." Armin was standing behind Micah, looking over his shoulder.

"Thanks, Armin."

"I mean, that turtle trying to jump through a hoop of fire really speaks to me. It's saying, 'Can I make it through the fire this time, or am I gonna get burned again?'" He nodded silently. "It's so true it hurts. You know what I mean?"

"Yeah, I think I know what you mean," said Micah. It wasn't a complete lie. But it mostly was. Is it a lie if you really hope it's true? He had no idea how guilty he should feel about this sort of fib.

Micah looked over at the painting on the easel beside him. It was the sort of thing Rembrandt could have painted when he was on top of his game. Armin had made a Viking ship flying upside down over a blue and red–striped field, with a herd of dragons on the ground below, shaking their fists up at the sky. Micah had no idea what it was supposed to represent, but he couldn't help being impressed. Armin was by far a better artist than Micah. He was also a great neighbor in art class, always helping Micah when he needed it. But when it came to art, Micah rarely understood what Armin was talking about.

As usual, there was a half circle of awestruck girls around Armin's easel. "That's amazing, Armin!" admired Stella Buckheiser.

"Yeah, you really captured the anger of those dragons," Annie Veep piped in.

Katie Wong nodded thoughtfully. "I feel like I'm right there in the field, part of the picture."

"What do *you* think?" Armin looked over at Micah. He sounded like he sincerely wanted Micah's opinion, and Micah had no idea why.

"I like it!" said Micah. He felt like he should probably say something more. "The dragons are very lifelike. I think they represent . . . maybe a dream that you'll wake up from?"

Armin stared at his own painting for a moment, his eyebrows tight with concentration. Then he nodded slowly. "You really get me, don't you?"

Maybe he did. Micah wasn't sure, but he hoped it was true.

The semicircle of girls slowly moved away from Armin's easel. As they passed by Micah's, he heard giggles behind him. Loud enough for the whole class to hear, Stella said to Katie, "I have no idea what's going on in that one."

Katie laughed. "That's not a soul I'd want to search."

Looking at his own painting, Micah couldn't help but agree.

How to Make Deep, Metaphorical Art (Mix-and-Match)

I may not be good at it, but if there's one thing I've learned in class, it's how to create "deep, meaningful" art. And the deeper it is, the more abstract it can be, which is perfect for reluctant artists like me.

To choose a subject for your painting, pick a "thing" from the left column, an "action" from the middle column, and a "place" from the right column. Then, simply paint the "thing" doing the "action" in the "place." Afterward, when someone asks you what it means, look thoughtfully off into the distance and answer: "It's truth. Life. Everything." When they tell you they still don't get it, just nod sadly and say, "You will. Someday, you will."

Thing	**Action**	**Place**
Muskrat	Eating a sandwich	In a haunted kitchen
Spatula	Chasing a bear	On the forehead of a giant
Ball of string	Riding a unicycle	Under a floating hoverboard
Spinach	Untying spaghetti	Behind the moon
Elbow macaroni	Running with scissors	On top of a lampshade
Map of Wichita	Changing a tire	Between the pages of a cookbook
Two blue wigs	Coughing up a cucumber	In a bowl of cereal
Canteloupe	Laughing at the sun	On the end of a kite

Mr. Spinoza walked slowly from easel to easel, making comments quietly to each artist, sometimes pointing at a detail in their paintings and asking a question. He finally arrived at Micah's easel.

He stared for a while in silent meditation. Then, in a sort of whisper, he asked, "Is that a row of donuts?"

Micah was glad Mr. Spinoza spoke so softly.

"It's supposed to be a turtle."

"Oh." Mr. Spinoza nodded. "Where's the head?"

Micah pointed at the small circle sticking out of a larger one.

"And what is this really big, jagged circle?"

"A hoop. It's on fire."

Mr. Spinoza was silent again for what felt like an hour. At last, he spoke, even softer than before. "Are you sure you're right-handed?"

"Pretty sure."

"Maybe mix things up and try your other hand for a while."

Micah sighed. It looked like another C– was in his future.

That afternoon, Micah did his chores and ate dinner, then biked over to school to meet Lydia and Armin in the music room. It was Friday, and that meant no homework! Normally, he wouldn't dream of spending time at school after hours (and on a weekend, no less!), but he was *desperate*.

As he walked past the auditorium, he could see Miss Petunia showing a dance move to a boy dressed as a burrito. Micah walked quickly and tried not to make eye contact. It was easy to get sucked into Miss Petunia's crazy world.

But that wasn't the plan for today. Today Lydia was going to see if Micah had any hidden musical talent beyond his early success with the triangle.

"Hi, Micah," Lydia greeted him with a hopeful smile.

"Hey, guys."

"Let's start by seeing if you can sing," she jumped right in. "Sing this scale: *do, re, mi, fa, so, la, ti, do!*"

"*Do, re, mi, fa, so, la, ti, do,*" he sang, dreadfully off-key.

"Not even close," said Armin.

Lydia shook her head. "Listen when I play the notes on the piano. Can you hear the difference?"

Micah nodded. He could hear it, all right. And he could hear the notes coming out of his mouth too. But he just couldn't seem to make the one match the other.

"Okay. Let's do something else. Are there any songs you already know the words to?" Lydia asked.

"I know the Erie Canal song from music class."

"Not exactly a crowd-pleaser," said Armin.

Lydia shrugged. "But let's give it a try."

Micah jumped right in. "*I've got a mule, and her name is Sal . . . fifteen miles on the Erie Canal.*"

He stopped when he heard loud footsteps coming into the room. Dennis, the janitor, was standing in the doorway. "What was that noise?"

"Micah was singing," Armin replied.

"Oh, that's good." Dennis was relieved.

"That was good?" Lydia wondered out loud.

"No. Definitely not," Dennis laughed. "I just meant good that it was only Micah singing. It sounded like a wounded animal. I thought I was going to have to pull a raccoon out of the air-conditioning vent again."

"Nope," said Lydia. "It was just Micah."

Dennis left with a shrug.

"How about we try the piano?" Lydia suggested. Under her breath, she added, "How bad can that sound?" Unfortunately, it was still loud enough for Micah to hear. He couldn't blame her—he really did sound awful, and they didn't seem to be getting any closer to figuring out his talent. Unlike Micah's sister, Lydia wasn't the sort of person who loved to criticize, so Micah realized she must be at her wits' end trying to help. He'd come to the end of his own wits some time ago, so he applauded her effort and patience.

Lydia sat at the piano bench, and Micah joined her. She played something intricate and beautiful. "That was Rachmaninoff. Do you know who that is?"

"Is he that squirrel who hangs out with that moose?"

"No, that's Rocky and Bullwinkle," Armin corrected.

"Oh."

"Just watch me," Lydia said.

Very slowly, she played a pretty melody of ten notes. "I'll do the same thing one more time, and then you can try it."

Micah watched carefully, trying to memorize where her fingers had gone.

"Okay. Your turn."

Micah tried. It sounded like nothing he'd ever heard. And not in a "groundbreaking feat of artistic genius" way. More in an "I don't ever want to hear that again" way.

"Not good, huh?" said Micah.

"I'm sorry, Micah. But no, it is not."

Armin shook his head. "You sound like someone humming a tune while falling backward down a flight of steps."

"That's not what I was going for," Micah admitted.

"No, I wouldn't think so," Lydia replied.

Step Away from the Awesome

Do you ever feel like it's harder to find out what you're good at when everyone around you seems to be so good at everything?!

I'm distracted by my friends' awesomeness! Like Armin and his art. It's one of *many* talents he has. I wish I could find just one of my own.

I have to admit, though, it's been fun to watch my friends do incredible things. I know I need to keep cheering them on, just like they've been doing for me.

So encourage each other and build each other up.
1 Thessalonians 5:11 (NLT)

> When other kids have BIG successes, does it make you feel SMALL, or are YOU able to cheer them on?

> Instead of comparing yourself to others, how can YOU be motivated by their gifts?

CHAPTER FIVE

Day: Monday

Time Until the Talent Show: 3 weeks, 3 days, 6 hours, and 22 minutes

What's Happening at School Today: Gym class (Ugh!)

As if Mondays weren't bad enough on their own, Mondays for Mrs. Grittner's fifth-grade class meant it was gym day. And this particular Monday meant there was only a little more than three weeks left until the talent show.

If fifth grade is a jungle—which seems about right—then gym class is the watering hole where all the animals gather in a small place and fight for survival. The battles take on different forms. Some are mostly painless, like kickball or playing with a parachute. Others demand every skill and instinct you have just to survive.

Today's game was dodgeball, the scariest jungle game of all.

The best athletes were a lot like cheetahs and lions—strong, fast predators always ready to take down their prey. The biggest kids in the class were elephants, hippos, and rhinos, milling about, waiting for the right moment to trample anyone in their path. Most of the other kids were zebras and wildebeests running in a herd as fast as they could, hoping that if they just stuck together, they might have a chance.

Micah, on the other hand, was like a meerkat— those skinny little pointy-nosed weasel-looking creatures that are always hiding in holes, looking terrified most of the time.

What Kind of Animal Are YOU?

Directions: Choose the number that best describes you. Then check the answers below to find out which animal you are.

1. Instead of going around things, I'd rather just run them over (trees, walls, little brothers, etc.).

2. I like to laugh at things other people don't find very funny, like big brothers running over little brothers.

3. I have a short temper, and charge without warning. And what are you looking at, anyway?

4. I'm a goofball and march to the beat of my own drum. Hey, look! Banana! What was the question again?

5. You can't see me. Please go away.

1. Elephant; 2. Hyena; 3. Rhinoceros; 4. Monkey; 5. Meerkat

All Micah wanted was to stay out of the way. He hung around toward the back wall, avoiding contact as much as possible.

Micah cautiously made his way to Armin and Lydia, who were in the other corner, also huddled near the wall.

"What is Gabe doing?" Lydia asked. Gabe, of course, was a monkey. He leaped and bounced and spun around like he was in a world of his own.

"I have no idea." Micah was at a loss.

"Do you think he even knows we're playing dodgeball?" Armin asked.

Lydia shrugged. "Hard to say."

Balls whizzed back and forth across the gym, thinning the herds as they picked off the weak and the slow.

A ball shot across the gym like a rocket. It came from Chet, the biggest, baddest dodgeball master of them all, and Micah watched it slam against Gabe's forehead before he could even shout a warning. It bounced so hard it hit the ceiling and ricocheted back down, taking out another kid in its path.

"Man down!" Gabe shouted. He lay there like a starfish, arms and legs spread out in every direction.

"Get up!" Armin yelled.

"I can't," Gabe croaked. "I'm dead."

"Nope," said Lydia to Micah and Armin. "He has no idea what game we're playing."

Armin nodded. "I'm going to pull him out."

Micah watched Armin duck down and rush to the middle of the court, grabbing Gabe by his legs to drag him to safety. Gabe might as well have really been dead. He lay limp on the floor, taking no part in his own rescue. Micah hurried out to help Armin.

As he grabbed Gabe's arms, Micah heard a shout and looked over his shoulder. Will Alameda was diving backward to catch a ball Chet had thrown, aimed right at Armin. Micah wasn't sure if Will had noticed him down there, and he had no chance of getting out of his way in time.

"Look out!" Will shouted.

With a crash of knees and shins, Will landed upside down on top of Micah. He'd tried to catch himself with his hands, but they bent backward as he fell.

"Sorry about that," Micah apologized as they untangled themselves. "I didn't mean to get in your way."

"Whatever," Will replied with a wince.

Micah knew this was not a "no problem" whatever. It was a "Why do you have to be so clumsy?" whatever. As Will got up to walk away, Micah could see he was weirdly holding both his hands. They didn't look right.

"What'd you do that for?"

"His wrists look really bad."

"Yeah. Smart move, blockhead."

"I'm guessing he did it on purpose."

"There goes the PB and J show! He's the cameraman, you know."

Still sitting on the ground, it took Micah a few moments to realize these remarks from his classmates were aimed at him.

"I didn't mean to trip him," he said quietly.

Out of nowhere, PB and J appeared, holding up their cell phones to get a video of Micah. Micah wondered how it was even possible to get a scoop this quick.

"Is that your official statement?" J asked.

"So, you're saying you weren't trying to trip up Will, but instead you're just that amazingly clumsy," PB said.

"Are you aware that as the cameraman for *The PB and J Report*, he is essential to the social fabric of the entire school?"

"Essential to the social what, now?" Micah asked.

"Do you have any comments for those who say you did this on purpose to sabotage our show?"

Micah sighed.

"Is that a 'no comment'?" asked PB.

"Sounds like a 'no comment' to me," said J.

Micah watched them walk away as he sat, stunned, on the gym floor. He could hear J talking to PB as they left.

"A 'no comment' is basically the same as admitting you're guilty."

That Thursday, after school, Micah went over to Armin's tree house. He climbed up the ladder through the hole in the floor to see Lydia, looking through Armin's paintings—mostly landscapes and animals, with a few video game monsters thrown in for good measure. Armin sat at his desk, with a paintbrush in his hand.

"Sorry about your rough day," Lydia said.

Micah shrugged. "I'm starting to get used to it."

"Well, let's try to turn things around," Armin said. "We can start by seeing if you can do anything with a hacky sack."

Armin pulled one out of his pocket and tossed it gently into the air, bounced it on one knee, then the other, then kicked it up to Micah.

Micah let it hit his stomach and roll down his body. Realizing this was not a great strategy, at the last second, he tapped it lightly with his toe. Actually, he tried to tap it lightly. Unfortunately, he lifted his leg at the same time as he tapped his toe, giving the hacky sack much more of a boost than he'd meant to. Up it flew, over his head, sailing in a huge arc until it hit the fan with a crash. A shower of beans flew across the tree house.

They all stood there for a moment in stunned silence.

"Do you have another one of those he could use?" Lydia asked.

"Yes, but I don't know if it's worth the risk," Armin said.

"I'll be all right," said Micah.

"I'm not worried about you. I'm worried about the hacky sack. And the fan. And my paints. And my paintings. And my—"

"Okay," said Micah. "You've made your point."

"Let's go outside," suggested Armin with a sigh. "We can try some juggling."

"I guess there's less to break out there," said Lydia.

Armin nodded. "We should go to the park across the street. That way we can stay away from windows."

Gabe was at the park, swinging by himself. "Hey, guys!"

"Hey, Gabe," Micah said.

Armin nodded at Gabe. "We're trying to teach Micah to juggle."

"Actually, Armin is teaching him to juggle," Lydia corrected. "I'm just here for moral support."

"I still think yo-yoing is the way to go!" said Gabe. He pulled his yo-yo out of his pocket and flipped it down and up and back and forth. "Here's a new one I'm working on."

He spun around in a circle while trying to yo-yo in the same spot, twisting his arm around himself. After two twists he caught his left foot against his right leg and started to fall forward. The yo-yo flew up in the air and slammed into his forehead.

"At least you didn't hit me this time," said Lydia.

Gabe looked at her in awe. "You *are* good at moral support."

Armin pulled three small balls out of his jacket pocket. He started to juggle slowly. "See, you toss the balls gently up in the air, then catch them one at a time. The trick is to be able to always focus on the one you're catching and throw it quickly without thinking about it."

Micah watched him in wonder. "Okay. I'll give it a go."

At first, he tried with just two balls. After much concentration, he was barely able to catch and toss them to himself. Then Armin tossed a third ball into the mix.

Micah panicked.

Now, if Micah had thought about it logically, he'd have realized there was no good reason whatsoever to panic. What difference did it make, after all, if the balls dropped to the ground? But for some reason, panic he did.

All three balls flung out of his hand like they were shot from a pirate's cannon. The first landed harmlessly twenty feet away, just past the swing set. The second nearly took out Armin's eye, but he ducked just in time—probably because he knew this was likely to happen.

But the third ball, that was the one to watch. It flew highest of all, thirty feet in the air toward a towering oak tree. At first, Micah was relieved they'd chosen to come to the park—a tree was much better than a window. But as he watched the ball shoot toward the oak's branches, he realized the squirrel the ball was about to hit was likely to disagree. It would have preferred the window.

Smack.

The squirrel took the ball right in the chin.

Smack. Smack. Smack.

On his way to the ground, the squirrel walloped branches with his rump, his back, and his left ear.

"Is he alive?" Lydia asked as they walked toward the fallen beast.

76

In answer, the squirrel hopped back onto its feet, gave each of them a dirty look, and scurried right back up the tree.

"I think I'm just going to go home now," said Micah. "This was fun," he added, not meaning it at all.

"Actually, it kind of was," Lydia said. "We have some great stories to tell." Then she looked at Micah's crestfallen face. "Or not."

What Have I Done?!

Not only am I UNTALENTED; this week I proved I'm a complete KLUTZ! I didn't mean to trip Will in gym class. I was actually trying to help Armin. But all anyone saw was me making a mess out of our dodgeball game, and now, Will could be really hurt.

I can't believe some kids think I did it on purpose. I didn't do it on purpose . . . did I? Why would I want to hurt Will?

This week stinks! I wish I could just be someone else . . . at least until the talent show is over . . . like Captain Karate Dino Cop fighting off the clan of evil robot pirate ninjas! Man, that would win me the talent show for sure! But who am I kidding? I'm no captain or dinosaur or cop . . . I'm just Micah.

Seems like my life can't get any worse at this point . . . Maybe next week will be better. I need something—anything—to go right so I don't feel like a total loser.

Don't be discouraged, for I am your God.
I will strengthen you and help you.
Isaiah 41:10 (NLT)

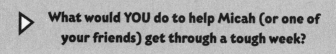

▷ Have YOU ever had a very, very bad week when it seemed everything was going wrong?

▷ What would YOU do to help Micah (or one of your friends) get through a tough week?

CHAPTER SIX

Day: Wednesday

Time Until the Talent Show: 2 weeks, 1 day, 5 hours, and 33 minutes

What's Happening at School Today:
Technology class (my favorite!)

Before he could plunge himself into the world of technology, Micah had to get through reading. His class was on chapter 5 in the three-headed alien book. The action was picking up. The good aliens in the Helion Galaxy were in a war against the evil aliens of Xenatron. Zargon, Blarnok, and Steve were trapped behind enemy lines!

Zargon still argued with Steve every chance he got because Steve was not particularly brave or tough, but Blarnok was starting to realize their third head came in handy. As it turned out, Steve was the only head with a sense of direction. If they were ever going to get out of there, they'd need to rely on Steve. But first, Steve needed to be able to focus without Zargon always breathing down his neck.

"Lydia, what do you think this chapter is about?" asked Mrs. Grittner.

Micah knew Lydia always had an answer. "The primary plot is obvious—in order to survive, they have to learn to trust one another, knowing that they each have important skills. But the subplot centers around the theme that none of us are truly independent in this hyperconnected world."

"Very interesting! And Chet, what do you think?"

"I think Lydia should use less nerd words."

Mrs. Grittner glared at him. "That's not very helpful. Just because you don't understand a term doesn't make it a 'nerd word.' Gabe, what did you think?"

Gabe looked up in surprise, thrilled to be asked a question. "I like space!"

"Okay," said Mrs. Grittner. "Could you expand on that idea?"

"Space is the best!" Gabe continued. "It's big with bright stars and planets and moons and black holes and comets and asteroids, but I can't remember if asteroids are real or just in video games, and shooting stars are my favorite, except when they fall to earth and land on people's heads, but usually they just—"

"That's enough expanding, Gabe. Thank you for, uh . . . participating."

Micah tried to read Mrs. Grittner's face. Confusion? Irritation? Exhaustion? If this were a test, he figured she'd choose "all of the above." He couldn't imagine trying to teach reading to fifth graders. Who wanted to talk about books anyway, when you could talk about video games? Or play them, for that matter? That's where the real action was.

". . . Micah?" Mrs. Grittner was asking.

Startled, Micah suddenly found himself blurting out words: "*Captain Karate Dino Cop.*"

Rats.

The whole class broke out in laughter.

"What did Mrs. Grittner ask me, anyway?" Micah whispered to Lydia.

"She asked what character in the story you're most like."

Double rats.

The bell rang. Finally! Technology time.

The computer lab was the one place in the whole building where Micah almost felt at home. He wasn't some sort of programming genius or anything, but he did know his way around a keyboard. Maybe it was all the video games he played, but Micah felt like he could usually get a computer to do what he wanted. Unlike people. Or musical instruments. Or a paintbrush. Or a hacky sack. Or a dog.

Okay, no need to rehearse the list of things he couldn't do. That was Mr. Turtell's job. Who, as it turned out, just happened to be filling in today for the normal lab teacher.

Mr. Turtell: always there for you when you need someone to ruin a good thing.

This week in computer lab they paired up with partners for video interviews. Lydia was Micah's partner, and they'd already asked each other questions on camera. Now they were editing the video they'd shot.

Micah was in the middle of showing Lydia how to use something called a "dissolve" to transition from her interview to his. "Not bad, Micah! That almost looks professional."

"Thanks! I kind of like it myself." This was the one class where Micah felt like he could actually teach Lydia a thing or two.

"Let's go back to the part where you talk about your family," said Lydia, rewinding the video.

"It's so hard to watch myself!" Micah cringed. "Even when playing back my vlog! Do I really sound like that?"

"Yes," said Hanz from the next computer over. "You really do sound like ze duck with ze head cold."

Micah tried to ignore him. Why must Hanz always hit him where it hurt?!

Armin, on the other side, tried to change the subject. "So, Micah, have you thought any more about what you're going to do for the talent show?"

"No! And I'm running out of time. There are only two weeks left! I should have just begged Miss Petunia to let me drop out. But I really want that new game system, and I'm not gonna lie: it would be nice to discover something I'm good at."

"Maybe tonight Lydia and I can come over to your house and help you think it through."

"Sounds good. I'm completely out of ideas."

"Have you tried magic yet?" asked Lydia. "Or

telling jokes?"

"At least I couldn't hurt anybody doing either of those things."

Armin nodded thoughtfully. "We'll be sure to keep you away from tricks that involve sawing people in half."

Mr. Turtell walked over to see what Lydia and Micah had done so far. "Not bad!"

Micah smiled. Finally, encouraging words from a teacher!

"Micah, you sure are lucky to be partnering with Lydia in this class."

"Actually . . ." Lydia started.

"You're right," Micah interrupted. "I am lucky." He figured it was a lost cause to try to convince Mr. Turtell that he was good at something.

The doorbell rang. Rats! Micah sprang out of his favorite chair in his bedroom and rushed as fast as he could to the front door. What had he been thinking, inviting friends over and then forgetting to get to the door before his dad? His dad was sure to tell his friends some embarrassing joke that hardly made any sense, and then Armin and Lydia would have to stand there and smile awkwardly.

He heard his dad's deep voice. "Ah! Somebody took a bite out of a 3 Musketeers bar!"

Too late. Micah hurried into the room just in time to witness their painful post-joke confusion.

"You get it?" said his dad. "Because you three are like a 3 Musketeers candy bar. But with only two of the three of you standing there, it's like someone bit off a third of the candy bar!"

"Yeah, I get it," said Armin with a forced grin.

Micah nodded, trying to smile himself. "We're going to go out to the backyard."

"Okay. Have fun and watch out for ants," Micah's dad said. "Because, you know, they like candy and sugar and stuff."

Micah hurried his friends out the back door before any more pain was inflicted. Barnabas followed them outside, and they all headed for the shade of the big maple tree, Micah's favorite thinking spot.

"I've got a deck of cards," Micah said. "And I looked up a trick online!"

He shuffled the cards as best he could. He only had to pick up four or five that fell out of his hand—his best shuffle ever! He fanned out the deck and held it up to Armin. "Okay. Pick a card and memorize it."

Armin picked one.

Micah shuffled again, cut the deck, swung the cards behind his back, and shuffled one more time. Then he selected a card from the top of the deck. "Was this your card?"

"No."

Micah shrugged. He picked the next one. "How about this?"

"No."

"This?"

"No."

He went through every single one. Nothing. The cards had betrayed him. He looked at the deck with the disappointment of someone who'd thought they had a chocolate chip cookie only to discover it was oatmeal raisin.

"Ugh. I don't get it. Where could it be?"

Armin shook his head slowly and held up the card. "It's still in my hand, Micah. You never asked for it back."

"Oh. I must've skipped a step."

Lydia nodded, a complete absence of surprise on her face. "I don't think you'll be able to focus any better when hundreds of students and their parents are staring at you. I say we move on to comedy."

"But I'm really not very funny."

"No argument here," said Lydia. "But we're running out of options."

Armin pulled a small, beat-up book out of his pocket. "Luckily I brought a secret weapon! This joke book had my sister and me laughing the entire drive to Sheboygan last spring break. I highlighted some great ones for you."

How to Tell a Dad Joke

Do you want to tell great dad jokes, but you think you're not old enough? Nonsense! Are you years away from even thinking about becoming a dad? Who cares! If you follow these simple steps, you'll soon be telling dad jokes with the best of them (like mine)!

- Always start with a pun. Puns are the building blocks of all good dad jokes.

- Try your best to ruin the punch line. Maybe forget an important word, or consider messing up the timing, telling the punch line before the setup.

- Explain your joke. This is key. Whether your audience gets the joke or not, always explain why it's funny. Nothing improves a joke like explaining it!

- Follow your joke with a ridiculous phrase like "That's a real knee-slapper!" or "I'm just pulling your leg." Then, of course, slap someone's knee and/or pull their leg. This never fails to win over the crowd.

See? Just like that, you're ready to tell dad jokes of your own.

Micah leafed through it. "Should I memorize some or just read them?"

"You've got to memorize them," said Lydia. "No one wants you to read to them from the stage."

Micah read several jokes to himself while Lydia and Armin waited. Finally, he landed on one he thought he could memorize.

"Which animals on Noah's ark didn't come two by two?"

"I don't know," said Armin. "Which ones?"

"The worms!" said Micah. "They came in apples."

Lydia stared at Micah.

Armin stared at Micah.

Barnabas stared at Micah.

"I don't get it," Lydia said.

Armin grabbed the book out of Micah's hand. "Let me see that." He skimmed over the page until he found the joke. "The animals came in 'pairs,' Micah. Not 'two by two.'"

"But it means exactly the same thing! I don't get it."

"Clearly," Lydia said.

Micah sighed. "So, I can't tell jokes or do magic or play an instrument or sing or hacky sack or juggle or anything. The talent show is two weeks away, and I'm hopeless. I've got to win that Ultra Game-A-Tron 64! It's the only way I'll ever get my hands on one!"

No one could think of anything to say, so they all just sat in the shade in silence. Micah stared sadly down at the grass until Barnabas licked his face to try to cheer him up.

"You could always try the mime thing," Lydia said.

"Ha!" laughed Armin. "At least then you wouldn't have to talk."

"Not funny," Micah said.

Armin shrugged. "Funnier than your joke."

Out of nowhere, Micah's face lit up like he'd just solved a difficult math problem with fractions, decimals, and maybe even a square root or two. "Oh!" he shouted. "Now I get it! Pairs! Pears! Hey, that's pretty good!"

Feels Like Me

Say what you want about my dad's lame jokes . . . at least he tells them right.

It seems like everything I try fails miserably. Shouldn't my talent be something I enjoy? I don't think my talent should feel forced . . .

Let's see . . . think, think, think . . . What are some things that I like?

I KNOW! I love pizza! Maybe eating pizza can be my talent! But EVERYONE loves to eat pizza. Well, except for Mr. Turtell.

Or . . . playing *Captain Karate Dino Cop*! That's something I love to do. But I always get stuck on level 6 (it's the level on a flying ninja pirate ship, where enemies throw chickens that twirl nunchucks. It's not easy!).

I do like making these vlogs. I don't know why. I guess I feel like I can be myself when I talk to the camera (though I don't always love watching myself). Maybe this is what I'm good at . . . but I can't see how this would work in a talent show.

Do everything in the name of the Lord Jesus, giving thanks to God the Father through him.
Colossians 3:17 (ESV)

▷ **Have YOU ever wondered why you're good at some things and not others?**

▷ **What things do YOU love to do?**

CHAPTER SEVEN

Day: Thursday

Time Until the Talent Show: 7 days, 5 hours, and 7 minutes

What's Happening at School Today: Hash Day (Yuck!)

Thursday was turnip hash day in the cafeteria. Turnip hash tasted about as flavorful as snow on the side of a highway. Micah would have loved to bring some spices from home to see if he could make it edible, but Mr. Turtell forbade any flavor experiments.

Armin, Lydia, and Gabe were already seated at a table when Micah came over to join them.

"So?" Armin asked Micah. "Are you any closer to getting that Ultra Game-A-Tron 64?"

Micah tried his best to swallow the turnip hash in his mouth. "I assume you're talking about my impossible task of finding a talent good enough to win the show?"

"Yep."

"Then nope."

Unfortunately, Mr. Turtell happened to be passing by and overheard their conversation. "Though I still refuse to get you out of it, I'd be glad to help. Let's see . . . where did we leave off? You can't swallow swords, you can't train falcons, you can't make shadow puppets, you can't breathe fire . . ."

A startled look came over Mr. Turtell's face. "Wait a second. Did Hanz bring his own pepper grinder?! What is happening around here?"

"Okay," said Lydia as Mr. Turtell rushed away to prevent a lunchroom catastrophe. "The talent show is only one week away. We've got to be logical about this. Let's think. When you really get yourself in a jam and can't see a way out, what do you need to do?"

"Run away?" Micah asked.

"Go into witness protection?" Armin asked.

"Become a pirate?" Gabe asked.

Lydia rolled her eyes. "Those are all terrific suggestions. Really, they are. But I was thinking about something more like coming clean to Miss Petunia. Throw yourself at her mercy. Let her know you don't have any talent. At all. I mean absolutely nothing. Not even the start of something we could work with—"

"Okay! We get your point," Micah said.

"Anyway, you've been seeking the help of the wrong teacher. Let Miss Petunia know you can't do the show. Surely she'll let you out of it."

"What if she just says no?"

"So what if she does?" Lydia asked.

Armin nodded. "Yeah, what's the worst thing

that could happen? You'd be in the same spot you're in now."

"Miss Petunia's goal is to see every student get up onstage and perform something during their time here at New Leaf Elementary. She might just make me stand up there in a crazy costume and do nothing, or worse, help her announce the acts."

Micah realized he'd be doomed no matter what.

"And if she says yes, I've lost all hope of that new game system. Either way, I lose."

The bell rang, driving the herd outside to recess. Micah grabbed his tray and stood up. "I guess I'll give it a try."

As they walked out the door, they could see Mr. Turtell posting a "No Unauthorized Spices" memo on the bulletin board, all the while mumbling to himself, ". . . and he can't win a hot dog–eating contest, and he can't win a pie-eating contest, and he can't play the steel drums, and he can't play the didgeridoo, and he can't be a human cannonball, and he can't tap-dance, and he can't break-dance, and he can't do the boogie-woogie . . ."

Micah walked to Miss Petunia's class after school. He felt like a lobster that had been yanked out of the beautiful ocean and tossed into a pot of boiling water. But for the lobster, it would be a quick ending. Micah felt like his doom might take a while.

"Oh, Micah!" Miss Petunia greeted him. "To what do I owe the pleasure?"

"I'm so sorry, Miss Petunia, but I made a huge mistake by signing up for the talent show."

"I think that's wonderful, Micah! I've always known you were a performer at heart."

"But the thing is, I don't actually have a talent."

"Nonsense!"

"No, really. We checked."

"Can you dance?"

"No."

"Everyone can dance."

"Not me."

"Aren't there any dances you know?"

"I know the chicken dance."

"You mean the one everyone does at the roller rink where they flap their arms like chicken wings? I love that one! Let's see it."

Micah gave it a go, singing the tune out loud as he did the hand motions, arm motions, and twisting motions. When he got to the part where he was supposed to grab a partner and swing her around, he held out his arm to Miss Petunia. She waved him off.

"You were right."

Lyrics to "Do the Micah"

(Warning: I recommend not doing this dance in front of other people unless they forgot their glasses at home or love you very much.)

Flap your elbows slowly while you sing a silly song

Tap your feet and try to get the beat completely wrong

Twist around, upside down, and shake out your caboose

Spin your head in circles 'til it's almost coming loose

Squeeze your feet and rub them like your toes are going numb

Investigate your pockets like you're searching for some gum

Clap with just your right hand while the left one's in the air

You don't know how to do this? Then you're almost halfway there!

"I was?"

"I thought everyone could dance! You cannot dance. Your arms look like a fish flopping around on the deck of a boat. And your legs? Oh, the humanity! I've seen bridges collapse more gracefully than what your legs were doing just then. Is something wrong with you? Do you have a sharp rock in your shoe? If you're injured, I could get the nurse."

"No. I'm fine. I just can't dance."

Miss Petunia shook off her look of concern, and enthusiasm reappeared on her face. "Can you sing?"

"I'm a better dancer than I am a singer."

"Okay," Miss Petunia said. "I probably don't want to hear that."

They both thought in silence for a while.

"Have you tried singing while dressed like a vegetable?" Miss Petunia asked. "Maybe a rutabaga? Or a summer squash?"

"I don't think that would help."

"Sadly, I think you're probably right."

Her eyes lit up. "Actually, maybe I do have

something you could do! Yes, this is the perfect way for you to stay involved. Do you know how to use a video camera?"

"I guess so . . . I have this video blog I've been working on."

"Marvelous! I need someone to make the video for the talent show! We were going to use Will Alameda, PB and J's cameraman, but he sprained his wrists in gym class."

Micah felt himself flush. He had no idea Will's accident was this bad, and it was all his fault. "I'm sorry to hear that."

"Anyway, there's no way he can do all that camera work with both his wrists in braces. So, I'd love for you to shoot the video and edit it. You'd be perfect!"

"Are you sure? I've only ever done my vlogs."

"Well . . . you're my only option. So, yes! I believe in you!"

"Um . . ."

"I've been looking for someone to fill in for him for weeks, and no one's volunteered. We want to have something to sell to all the parents and anyone else who wants it. We're always looking for ways to raise money for the drama club!"

"It sounds like a big responsibility."

"I'm sure you'll do great. Besides, if you want to get out of performing, this is your only option." She grinned her biggest grin, and her eyes lit up behind her glasses.

"Well . . ." Micah paused. This would mean there was absolutely no chance of winning the Ultra Game-A-Tron 64. He wanted the new gaming system so bad! But he still hadn't found anything he could do for the show, so what choice did he have?

"Okay. I guess."

"Excellent!" Miss Petunia said.

Micah was absolutely terrified. The talent show was only a week away! His vlog was a one-man show. It was easy to record and edit. How could he possibly learn everything else he needed to know about making a professional video that quickly?

But he also felt something else. What was this? Hope? Excitement? It had been so long since he'd felt either one.

A Glimmer of Hope

Today I asked Miss Petunia if I could drop out of the talent show. It wasn't easy! I was sure that she was going to force me into getting onstage in some sort of fruit costume. And dropping out would mean giving up my one and only chance of getting the Ultra Game-A-Tron 64 (even if that chance was slim).

At least now I don't have to perform (phew)! All I have to do is tape the performance and edit a video that will be sold to the entire school! That means teachers, students, and parents will watch this video. Seems pretty important!

I had no idea when I started playing around with the vlog thing that it could lead to something more. I don't want to get ahead of myself. This is a big job, and I'm not completely sure I know what I'm doing. But I have a good feeling about this . . .

May the God of hope fill you with all joy and peace as you trust in him.
Romans 15:13 (NIV)

▷ **What do YOU think would help Micah with his fear and uncertainty?**

▷ **What is something YOU do well that could have bigger purpose in your life?**

CHAPTER EIGHT

Day: Saturday

Time Until the Talent Show: 5 days, 9 hours, and 30 minutes

What's Happening ~~at School~~ Today: No one is really sure . . .

Saturday morning, bright and early, Micah found himself biking down a road he barely knew. He didn't recognize any of the street signs or buildings. Where was he, anyway? Did the people around here speak the same language as him? Did they eat weird foods? Did they use the same money?

At last, there it was, the building Micah had been looking for. Who would've thought that of his own free will, he would ever visit the library!

Micah parked his bike against one of the white columns and entered the big wooden doors. As soon as he walked inside, he felt as if he had somehow stepped outside of time. What was that horrible noise? He listened very closely until he finally recognized it: silence.

He could feel the presence of books thinking evil thoughts at him, like, "You're not welcome here," and "Go back to your video games, where you belong!"

On Micah's right was a statue of a thinker hunched over her desk. It looked so real he could almost see her shoulders rise and fall as she breathed.

The statue sneezed.

That was about the time it crossed Micah's mind that perhaps it wasn't, in fact, a statue. Yep, it was just a regular old human who spent way too much time reading and didn't even bother to leave the library for naps. Micah promised himself he would never be like that.

The woman trembled with a loud snore, and Micah moved along quickly.

He'd just put his backpack down on a table when he was startled by a whisper. "What are you doing here?"

Micah turned around to see Lydia staring at him in wonder.

"I need to do some research."

"I didn't know you even knew the word 'research,' let alone how to do it."

"Of course I do!"

"Are you grounded from video games or something?"

"No." He was a little annoyed by the question, but he couldn't really blame her. "I just need to figure out how to make a video."

Lydia was surprised. "A video? What for?"

"I went to talk to Miss Petunia like you suggested. Instead of letting me out of the show, she asked me to record and edit a video of the whole thing." Micah's stomach became queasy as he said it out loud.

"Wow. I was wondering how it went with Miss Petunia. That's great, Micah," Lydia said. "But I thought you already knew how to make videos. I'm your partner in the computer lab, remember? And what about your vlog?"

"Yeah, but for the talent show I'm supposed to use multiple cameras and several microphones," Micah replied, trying not to sound too unsure of himself. "I have to edit the whole thing together into something Miss Petunia can actually sell!"

"What's that look on your face?" Lydia asked. "You look scared, of course, but there's something else. It almost looks like you're . . . you're excited."

"Maybe I am," Micah admitted with a half grin. "Remind me what excitement feels like again?"

"Sort of like you have a lot of extra energy, but not the terrified kind where you want to run away. It's the kind that makes you get up early and work hard at something."

"Huh. Then yeah, I guess I'm excited."

Lydia smiled. "Then let's not waste it! Let me show you how to use the Dewey decimal system!"

Micah winced. "I heard that's even more

confusing than the regular decimal system."

"Yeah! It's awesome!"

Soon Micah had a big stack of books beside him, and he began to read all about making professional-looking videos. The silence didn't sound so bad anymore. It actually helped him concentrate on the words. And what was more, the books were interesting. The library was full of surprises. Could learning be fun? Was this what Lydia's life was like?

Micah couldn't believe how hungry he was at dinner that night, and everything tasted amazing. The mashed potatoes were as fluffy as heaven's clouds, and he could have written a sonnet about the baked chicken—if he could just remember what a sonnet was.

"This chicken is delicious, Mom."

"Thanks, honey!"

"What's gotten into you?" Audrey asked him. "It's not even fried."

His mom ignored her and looked at Micah. "So, what did you land on for the talent show, kiddo?"

Micah hadn't told them the news yet and wasn't sure how they'd react. "Actually, I got out of it."

"Smart move on Miss Petunia's part," Audrey said. "Your performance could have made somebody ill or maybe even sparked a revolution. It was a lawsuit waiting to happen."

"Don't listen to your sister, Micah," his dad said. "It's the school's loss."

His mom got up from the table to fill up Micah's milk glass. "So, where have you been all day? You left early this morning, and I don't think we've seen you since."

"I was at the library."

Everyone stopped chewing. Audrey froze with her fork halfway to her mouth.

"Are you feeling all right?" his mom asked.

"Did I forget that we grounded you from video games?" his dad wondered aloud.

"The end is near!" Audrey exclaimed. "We need to build a bunker and start gathering canned goods!"

Micah shook his head. "Everything's fine. Instead of performing in the talent show, I'm going to be recording and editing the video."

More silence from Micah's family.

"I'm actually kind of excited. I went to the library to research how to do it."

Micah's mom beamed. "I'm so proud of you, honey!"

"That's all well and good," Audrey whispered loudly to her mom. "But it would be smart to keep our eyes out for any signs of alien mind control."

Their mom refused to stop grinning. "Well, if the aliens make you become a bookworm and appreciate my baked chicken, then I'm all for it."

His dad scooped up a spoonful of peas from his

plate. "I guess the aliens come in peas! Get it? Come in 'peace'?"

Micah caught a glimpse of a smile on his sister's face. At first, he thought it was at his dad's joke, but that was impossible. Could she actually be a little proud of him?

By Monday Micah was feeling pretty good about his research, so that meant it was time to actually try out what he'd learned. And that meant hanging out at school in the computer lab after hours.

Micah was right in the middle of trying to figure out how to edit together video from two different cameras when Dennis walked by.

"What are you doing here?" Dennis asked.

"I'm working on a project."

"Are you grounded from video games or something?"

Micah sighed. "No."

"Are you writing your name all over the desk?"

"Nope."

People Who Are Still at School at 5:00 p.m. on a Weeknight

- Chet, who fell asleep in detention and hadn't woken up yet.

- Dennis, the janitor, who was cleaning up from the food fight in the lunchroom. (Someone had foolishly served "everything" bagels.)

- Miss Petunia, gleefully making a giant winter squash costume.

- Gabe, who accidentally locked himself in a janitor closet sometime before lunch.

"Putting chewing gum under the chair?"

"Nope."

"Taking all the gum that's already under the chair and stretching it across the window to make a giant spiderweb?"

"No. That's disgusting."

"Sticking pencils into the ceiling?"

Micah thought this one actually sounded like a fun idea. But maybe later. "Nope."

Dennis squinted his eyes for a few moments. "Carry on."

Micah had no idea where the time went, but it was 6:30 p.m. when Miss Petunia came in. "Sorry, Micah, but you're going to have to leave now. I have to lock up the lab and go home."

"Thanks for letting me use it for a while," Micah said.

"Absolutely! I looked in on you a couple times, and you actually looked like you were enjoying yourself! I'm sure it's not as fun as singing to the back of the room while dressed like an enormous burrito, but we can't all be performers!"

Micah had never worked so hard in his life. But at the same time, Miss Petunia was right—he was enjoying himself!

Who Knew?

This weekend I did the unthinkable! I went to the library . . . on a SATURDAY!

You'll never guess who I saw there . . . Okay, maybe it's obvious. Lydia was in her element, surrounded by books and knowledge. At first I felt like I didn't belong, like the books themselves were shunning me. But after a while I sat down and focused on what I needed to do: I had to make a video, and I had to make it good.

I got a glimpse of what Lydia's life is like, and I have to admit . . . I didn't hate it. It felt great to focus, to research and learn more about something I'm interested in.

I may not be good at math or science, like Lydia, but maybe God made me good at other things. Who knew the library could help me learn . . . about myself?!

For we are God's masterpiece. He has created us anew in Christ Jesus, so we can do the good things he planned for us long ago.
Ephesians 2:10 (NLT)

 Why do YOU think Micah is finally enjoying learning?

 What can YOU focus on that might help you see yourself differently?

CHAPTER NINE

Day: Thursday

Time Until the Talent Show: 0 days, 0 hours, and 10 minutes. It's showtime!

What's Happening at School Today: Duh?! The talent show!

The PB and J Report had set up camp just to the right of the stage to do their big "Pre-Show Red Carpet Extravaganza." Micah was only a few feet away, doing a last-minute check of one of his own cameras. Without Will as their cameraman,

PB and J had to use their cell phone and a selfie stick.

"Are you ready, PB?"

"I'm ready, J!"

"You better be! This is going to be the event of the year!"

"Of the decade!"

"Of the century!"

"I have to stop there because I can't remember what comes after century!"

"Okay, PB! But let me ask you this: Have you ever witnessed such a collection of talent in one place?"

"Not as far back as I can remember, J! And I'm already eleven!"

"All this skill and artistry boggles the mind, PB!"

"My mind is blown, J!"

"There will be singing, dancing, juggling, magic yo-yoing . . ."

"I heard there may be a performing robot dog!"

"A robot dog?"

"That's right!"

"Wow! What a night!"

"It looks like Miss Petunia is about ready to take the stage. From all of us at *The PB and J Report*, I hope you enjoy the show!"

Micah was bent over, adjusting the angle of his camera's tripod, when something knocked into him from behind. He fell forward, collapsing the tripod. His camera tumbled to the floor.

He looked up to see PB glaring at him. "Aren't you the kid who tripped Will too? Can't you ever watch where you're going?"

"But you knocked into me," Micah said.

J shook her head. "Then you need to figure out how to stay out of everyone's way."

Micah stood up with the tripod and opened it back up, but he couldn't get one of the legs to stay in place.

He felt a tap on the shoulder. "Are you missing this?" It was Armin, holding up a small circle of plastic. I can help you get it back together."

"Thanks, man."

The tripod seemed to stand up fine once the ring

of plastic was back where it needed to be. Armin nodded at him. "The show is about ready to start. I should get backstage."

"Good luck, Armin!"

"You too, Micah!"

Armin was right. Immediately the curtain opened, and Micah pushed the record button on his camera just before Miss Petunia walked onto the stage. The two other cameras he'd set up were already recording—one far back in the center of the auditorium and one stage left.

"Students, parents, and faculty, welcome to the New Leaf Elementary School Fifth Annual Talent Extravaganza! You're in for quite a treat. Everyone has worked very hard on their acts, and I know you'll be impressed. In fact, a professionally edited video of the entire performance will be available a few days after the show for only $20. All proceeds will go to support the drama department and our upcoming musical, *Don't You Carrot All?*"

A wave of nervousness passed over Micah. He was responsible for the "professional-ness" of the video, and there was no backing out now. If he didn't deliver, not only would Miss Petunia be angry, but so would a lot of parents. Maybe even his classmates. But there was nothing to be done now. The cameras were set up and rolling. All he could do was watch the show.

Micah knew that Lydia, to her disappointment, would be the very first act. She strolled confidently onto the stage in a beautiful blue dress and played a Beethoven piece on the piano. Micah only knew it was Beethoven because she'd been talking about it for three weeks, and only knew she was nervous because she'd been talking about that for three weeks too. What he didn't know, even by the end of the song, was whether or not she'd messed up. She was so far beyond Micah in her talent and skill that her "mistakes" were hard for him to notice.

But when her song was over and she took her bow, the thrilled look on her face gave it away. She'd played the piece perfectly! Micah smiled up at her. She caught his eye and smiled back.

Miss Petunia came back onstage. "Thank you, Lydia! That was beautiful. For our next act, we have Chet Penter doing a strongman show. How exciting!"

Micah didn't know what they were in for.

Before Chet took the stage, three of his buddies rolled out a low platform on wheels with several blankets covering whatever was sitting on it. A rousing guitar riff filled the air, and Chet strolled out in a tank top and shorts. He flexed his biceps for the crowd, walked over to the platform, and yanked away one of the blankets.

Micah had no idea what to expect but wasn't expecting this. A mini fridge. With a flourish, Chet opened up the refrigerator door to reveal that it was filled with several six-packs of soda, a bag of frozen peas, and what looked like a large casserole.

Chet closed the door again and glared at the mini fridge for several seconds. Once he felt the small appliance had been intimidated enough, he reached down with both hands, grabbed it in a bear hug, and swung it up into the air. He held it in place above his head for several seconds until his arms and legs were shaking. Then, with a loud grunt, he dropped it onto the stage in front of him.

The crowd roared in approval. Even Micah couldn't help but be impressed. He had no idea how heavy a mini fridge was, but he'd carried his fair share of soda and casseroles.

For his second and final feat of strength, Chet's three buddies strolled back onstage and yanked a blanket from another object. The crowd gasped when they saw what it was. A sectional couch. All four of the kids onstage lifted the sofa off the platform and onto the floor, then rolled the platform out of the way. Then everyone but Chet piled onto the couch.

From ten feet away, Chet stared them down, much as he had the mini fridge. Then, with three deep breaths, he charged.

A mother rhinoceros protecting her baby could not have attacked a lion any more ferociously. The crowd gasped as the couch sailed across the stage like a hovercraft, Chet's buddies hanging on for dear life.

Before it even came to a complete stop, Chet swung himself over the top of the couch and pushed it back the other way.

Back and forth he went across the stage, faster and faster, until sweat was pouring down his forehead and the front of his tank top was dark from moisture.

The crowd loved every second of it! They cheered and screamed and stomped their feet. They were so loud Micah was surprised he could hear Dennis's low grumbling from behind. "That'll leave scratches. I hope they don't expect me to refinish the stage."

At last Chet gave the sectional one more, huge heave, sending it sailing offstage. Hands high in the air, he jogged up to the microphone and stared at the crowd.

"Just so you know. That couch has a hideaway bed."

And with that, he walked offstage.

Micah shrugged. Nope. He hadn't seen that coming.

The crowd went wild! You could hear the applause from two counties away. Lily McMichael clutched her heart. Rachel Hubbins collapsed on the ground, pretending to faint. No one had ever seen anything like it.

It took the audience a long time to settle back down, but at last Miss Petunia was able to get the show moving again. The next two performances were Renee Pickwick doing a tap dance routine and Mary DeStefano's magic act.

Mary's act ended with—wouldn't you know

it—a sawing-in-half routine. As Mary revealed to the shocked crowd that Liam Stover, her victim, was still alive and in one piece, all Micah could think about was how glad he was to not be up there onstage himself.

But as the gasps of the crowd quieted, and Mary and Liam walked offstage in triumph, Micah glanced over at his central camera. It stood near the wall at the back of the auditorium and was hard to see in the low light. Why did it look like it was angled up at the ceiling?

In a panic, he rushed behind the crowd over to the tripod. Sure enough, the camera was aimed completely wrong, not catching one bit of the stage. How had this happened? He'd checked it carefully three times before the show started and had tightened everything, so no one could accidentally knock it out of place.

Micah's gaze swept around him. He didn't know exactly what he was looking for. Answers, he supposed. Over to his left, his eyes landed on Will

Alameda. A tight grin came over Will's face as he stared right back at Micah. This was no accident. It was payback.

Micah felt awful. He was the reason Will couldn't make the video, and now here he was doing it himself. But he couldn't worry about that right now. He adjusted the camera back into place and tried to calm himself down. Two other cameras were catching most of the stage. Hopefully, he could make it all work out with editing.

But in the meantime, he'd need some backup.

"Hey, Micah. How's it going?"

Micah looked behind him to see Lydia grinning from ear to ear. Just in time!

"Lydia, you were absolutely amazing! I want to talk to you about it after the show. But right now, could you do me a huge favor?"

"Of course."

"Could you watch this camera and make sure it stays focused on the stage? I don't know why I didn't ask anyone to help me before."

"Glad to, Micah. And yes, that was silly of you."

"Thanks. I need to get back to the other camera on the right. And we can both keep an eye on the one on the left, just to make sure it doesn't move."

"Cameras move?"

"They do if someone moves them. I'll explain later."

From the stage, Miss Petunia announced that Armin was going to do a hacky sack routine. Micah headed back over to his camera to watch.

Armin started simple, kicking the hacky sack back and forth from one foot to another, getting into a rhythm. But then things got fancy. He flipped it up to his head and bounced it on a shoulder, then let it roll down his back. He kicked it up from behind him with his heel, over his head, and caught it on his knee. Then he did the exact same routine twice as fast as before!

Micah knew he was good, but he'd never seen him in such a rhythm.

But then, on the very last kick of his heel, the hacky sack flew over his head, bounced off his knee, and slid onto the ground. Micah knew it was supposed to land on his knee and stay there. But he didn't see a trace of disappointment on Armin's face.

In fact, Micah wondered if Armin would have been a little disappointed if he'd done everything perfectly. He was always pushing himself as hard as he could to try things he wasn't sure he could do. If he'd done the whole thing perfectly, he might have felt like he hadn't pushed himself hard enough.

Which, for him, meant it wasn't as fun. Micah admired that about him.

Miss Petunia was already announcing the next act. "Next up we have dog tricks with Hanz and his amazing robot dog!"

Hanz strutted onto the stage, followed by his robot dog, Pouncer, whom Micah disliked almost as much as its owner. It looked a bit like a Rottweiler, but shinier. And with more buttons.

Hanz held his remote control in the air and looked at the crowd to silence it. Then, with a flourish, he brought the remote back down and began pushing buttons. Pouncer leaped onto his front paws and began walking on them. Then he sat up, did a perfect cartwheel, danced what looked like the foxtrot, and, finally, jumped through a hoop that he held in his own mouth. How was that even possible?

For the final trick Pouncer used his teeth to reach into a small compartment in his body and pulled something out. It was hard to tell what it was at first, but when Pouncer stood up on his hind legs, held the

5 Things Hanz Could Do with Pouncer Besides Perform in a Talent Show

1. Enter a dog contest—I'm sure the judges would be enamored by his harmonica-playing abilities.

2. Try out for a dog food commercial—Doglicious Delights would be lucky to have that tin can as their mascot. Speaking of mascots . . .

3. Serve as the Middletown Mutts team mascot—though that poor petite girl that lives down the street would be out of a job . . .

4. Visit with the residents of the Middletown Retirement Community. Those sweet old ladies won't even realize he's a fake.

5. One word . . . RECYCLE.

object between his paws, raised it to his snout, and began to play, Micah realized it was a harmonica. It took a few notes before Micah recognized the song. Huh! "The Erie Canal." Figures.

Micah guessed Hanz was probably mocking him, but he didn't care. It was a great song. Micah hummed along, off pitch, of course.

After the song, Pouncer took a bow. Then Hanz took a bow, smiling proudly from ear to ear. Micah had no idea what he was so proud of. Maybe if you have a robot dog, his wins are your wins. Micah wouldn't know.

"Thank you, Hanz," Miss Petunia said. "That was most . . . interesting. It was also the last act before intermission. We'll have more exciting performances in fifteen minutes. Toodle-oo for now!"

Micah took a deep breath. Halfway there! He wondered what it would have been like to perform a talent, and maybe win the Ultra Game-A-Tron 64. But if he couldn't win it himself, at least his friends had a shot.

Armin and Lydia came over to join him. "You two both did amazing!" Micah told them.

"Thanks! I heard someone messed up one of your cameras," Armin said. "I hope it works out all right."

"We'll see, I guess." Micah shrugged. "I'm trying not to think about that right now."

Lydia nodded. "Well, you've gotten to see all the acts so far. Who do you think will win?"

"I have no idea, but I hope it's one of you two."

"Or maybe Gabe," Armin said.

Lydia shook her head. "I think it'll be a win for Gabe if he doesn't accidentally knock himself out with his yo-yo."

Sabotaged?!

I don't have much time. The talent show is going on right now! It's intermission, so I've only got a few minutes to collect my thoughts and get back out there. I just needed a moment to process it all. I can't believe someone would try to sabotage me like this. How could Will stoop so low as to try to ruin this video for everyone?!

It doesn't really matter. What matters is that I don't let it get to me and I go out there and finish what I started. Let's do this!

I can do all [things] through him who gives me strength. Philippians 4:13 (NIV)

▷ **What do YOU think Micah should do to stay focused on the task at hand?**

▷ **What would YOU do if someone tried to sabotage you?**

CHAPTER TEN

Gabe opened the show after intermission. Micah could feel a tingle of nerves in his own stomach. He wasn't expecting greatness or even okay-ness. He just hoped whatever happened, it would still be okay for them to be seen together in public.

Gabe came out to silence. No entrance song. No applause. No cheering fan club. With a look of concentration on his face, he started to yo-yo.

It started out simple. Up and down. Make it sleep. Around the world. Walk the dog. Just the basics. But by the grin on his face, Micah could tell he was pleased with himself.

A little embarrassing, but not humiliating. Micah guessed that would be it.

He was wrong.

Without warning, Gabe started spinning the yo-yo around his head like David about to slay Goliath. Faster and faster it went, and as it spun, Gabe started spinning too, twisting the yo-yo around his arms and legs as he went.

It was right around his knees where things took a bad turn.

Gabe didn't have great balance under the best of circumstances. Having the string of a yo-yo wrapped around your knees, elbows, neck, and left ear was not, it turned out, the best of circumstances.

Up went the yo-yo, aiming right at his head. Down went Gabe.

Unfortunately, by this time he found himself right on the very edge of the stage. There was nowhere to fall but down to the floor of the auditorium, five feet below. Heels overhead, he plunged to the ground in a tangled mess of string.

Micah just hoped he wouldn't be knocked out cold.

But then something happened that no one expected.

He landed on his feet.

The yo-yo whipped back around both knees, both elbows, his neck, and his right ear, and sprang back into his hand like he'd planned it that way all along. He stood there, hands high in the air like an Olympic gymnast who'd just stuck the best landing of his life. And then he smiled.

Micah knew it was all a complete accident. Maybe everyone did. But who cared? It was spectacular!

Micah jumped to his feet and clapped his heart out, not even looking around to see if anyone was joining him.

But they did. They couldn't help it! The crowd somehow yelled even louder than they had for Chet! The screams and shouts shook the whole room. Josh Jenkins started to hoot and holler. Rachel Hubbins fell to the ground again. It was hard to know for sure, but Micah thought it was for real this time.

Micah felt sorry for whoever was next. How could you follow something like that? Tina Dropp handled it bravely, break-dancing to a remix of the theme song from the *Harry Potter* movies. Then Miguel Soto read *Hop on Pop* as slam poetry.

The final act of the night was Frank Millwood. The auditorium was abuzz with anticipation. Micah was sure he'd do something amazing, which was the last thing he wanted to see.

Frank unicycled onstage. Everyone cheered.

Strangest Performances in New Leaf Elementary School's Talent Show History

- Austen Burkell jumping a stack of kindergartners
- DeAngelo Dalton playing "name that smell"
- Mia Abramowitz performing a reenactment of the signing of the Magna Carta with finger puppets
- Jamie Wang creating gummy worm caricatures of her favorite NBA players
- Julio Jimenez filleting a smallmouth bass with a paper clip and a #2 pencil

From backstage, someone tossed him a tennis ball. He caught it. Everyone cheered.

Another tennis ball was tossed into the mix. More applause.

Then another.

And another.

Four tennis balls now whirled around his head like he was some kind of giant electron. Then, to everyone's shock, a fifth ball appeared! And this one was a beach ball.

Still, the balls whirled, faster and faster, none hitting the ground.

Then, still juggling the tennis balls, Frank somehow grabbed the beach ball and balanced it on his nose. The crowd went crazy! How was he doing this? Boys shouted. Girls screamed. Grown women put their hands to their foreheads like they were going to faint.

But Frank still wasn't done!

Frank's friend Bobby Gingrich appeared from backstage, rolling out a table from the lunchroom.

On the table were five bowls. They looked like ingredients, but for what? Still unicycling, Frank put down the balls and approached the bowls. From the first bowl, he grabbed a crunchy taco shell. The crowd went crazy. Who doesn't love tacos?

He unicycled from one bowl to the next—meat, cheese, lettuce, and salsa. What was he up to? Was he really making a taco to eat in front of the whole crowd? What a mess!

Still unicycling, he took a bite.

Not one drop fell from the taco.

Then another bite.

Again, nothing dropped. Somehow the taco was still intact!

Another. Another. Still, not one drop of taco fixings had fallen to the ground!

Another.

One more.

Last bite!

He'd done it! Every bit of taco had gone into his mouth! He'd eaten the whole thing without any

spills! Almost no fifth graders had ever done such a thing in their whole lives, and Frank Millwood had done it riding a unicycle!

Such a feat as this deserved the admiration of kids all over the world. The applause thundered through the auditorium. They cheered on their hero with a standing ovation that seemed to last forever.

Now all that was left was to wait for the judging. To his surprise, Micah was nervous. He was sad not to have a chance to win the Ultra Game-A-Tron 64, but hopefully, it would go to a friend.

Miss Petunia stepped to the microphone. She held a small card in one hand and the Ultra Game-A-Tron 64 in the other. "The moment you've all been waiting for! I'm proud to announce the winner of the New Leaf Elementary School Fifth Annual Talent Extravaganza is . . ." She looked at the card in her hand. Was that a look of surprise on her face?

"Gabe Tompkins!"

The crowd roared again. Gabe was a smiler by nature, but as he came out to accept his prize, Micah thought his face might crack in half. He wasn't sure he'd ever seen such a grin.

Miss Petunia handed him the Ultra Game-A-Tron 64, and he held it high in the air like a boxer accepting the championship belt.

"Thank you all so much for coming," Miss Petunia said. "And don't forget to order your video of tonight's performance!"

As the applause died down, Gabe caught Micah's eye and headed toward him, aiming for the steps at the front of the stage. For some reason, Micah could see in his mind what was about to happen.

Sure enough, Gabe missed the edge of the first step.

He lurched backward, catching himself with his hands just before he hit the ground. Unfortunately, he'd been holding the Ultra Game-A-Tron in those hands.

Up it flew into the air.

Frank Millwood happened to be heading toward the stage to congratulate Gabe. To his surprise, an Ultra Game-A-Tron 64 greeted him first. Micah was too far away to help, but he had a front row seat to watch Frank leap sideways with all his might to catch the game before it hit the ground.

This was the first time Micah had ever rooted for Frank! Unfortunately, it was also the first time he'd ever seen him miss a catch. The Ultra Game-A-Tron 64 fell two inches from his outstretched fingertips.

Crestfallen, Gabe hurried over and picked it up. It rattled in a way only broken things can.

Gabe shook his head. He looked at Micah. "Sorry. I know we would have had fun playing with it together."

Micah smiled at him. "I know we would have. But you can come over and play with my old system whenever you want."

Win or Lose?

Gabe winning the talent show? Beating Frank and Chet and Hanz? Who would have thought?!

Too bad the Ultra Game-A-Tron 64 is completely ruined. Somehow, I don't think Gabe is bothered by that. He's probably just happy he (sort of) pulled off his yo-yo trick.

I guess winning isn't always about the prize. Maybe it's more about knowing you did your best, even if you lose. Hmmm . . . I guess losers can be winners too!

And we know that God causes everything to work together for the good of those who love Him. Romans 8:28 (NLT)

▷ **What do YOU think was more important to Gabe: the prize or the win?**

▷ **Why do YOU think that sometimes the prize isn't the real reward?**

CHAPTER ELEVEN

By the time Micah had his cameras all packed up, he and Dennis were the only ones left.

Dennis was looking up at the auditorium ceiling, thirty feet above their heads.

Micah looked up too. He could barely see skinny, yellow things sticking out of the ceiling tiles.

Dennis stared at Micah. "Did you throw those pencils up there?"

"I couldn't even throw one that high."

"So, then you've tried."

"No, I . . ." Micah thought whatever he would say would just make it worse, so he stopped talking.

As soon as Micah got home from school the next day, he went to work right away. Miss Petunia had given him the weekend to finish. He got out his library books and asked his mom if he could use their computer. When his dad found out about the video, he'd bought the software Micah needed, so he didn't have to go to the school lab anymore.

His mom came up behind him. "Need any help, honey?"

"No, I'm fine."

He got to work. He hadn't watched the recordings yet and was nervous. How was he going to deal with no central camera for the first few acts? Would it look ridiculous?

Oh, well. He'd have to work with what he had and make the best of it.

He'd learned a lot in the last week, but it still wasn't a quick job. He'd never focused so hard in his life, switching from camera to camera, making sure everything transitioned smoothly and there were no gaps.

The first few acts were the hardest to make look good, but he was figuring out how to switch the other cameras often enough to make it work. It wasn't what he would have chosen, but he didn't know if anyone else would notice.

The phone rang.

"Want to hang out?" Lydia asked.

"No, I'm in the middle of editing the talent show video."

"Okay. Just let me know if you can ride bikes later."

Next, Micah added music to open and close the

video and between acts. He knew he didn't have anything cool enough, so he grabbed some kind of retro-futuristic funk from Audrey's playlist. Stuff you couldn't hum to if you tried. Perfect.

The phone rang.

"Hey, man. Want to come over and play *Captain Karate Dino Cop 4* with me?" Armin asked. "My dad was so proud of my hard work on the hacky sack routine, he just bought me the new Ultra Game-A-Tron 64!"

"I told Miss Petunia I'd finish up the video. And actually, I'd kind of rather do that than play video

games right now anyway." Wow. He never thought he'd hear himself say that.

"Okay. Just say the word if you want to take a break and come over."

Back at it. Micah watched the whole video again, slowly trimming gaps in the action as much as he could to make it flow. He was amazed at how much dead time there was, and he found himself trimming off half a minute here and forty-five seconds there.

He heard someone come up behind him.

"No! I don't want to play right now!" Micah snapped. He looked over his shoulder and saw Barnabas standing there, tilting his head in confusion.

"Sorry, buddy. I didn't mean to snap."

He heard his dad come down the stairs. "Hey, Micah. It's time for bed. You've been burning the candle at both ends. Maybe in the middle too!" He laughed and slapped his own knee at his weird joke.

"Okay," Micah agreed. "I think I'm getting too worked up about it anyway. I'll get back at it tomorrow."

Micah lay in bed, not feeling at all tired. Not because he was worried or in trouble, as usual. But because he had a million ideas and wanted to get up early the next morning to try them.

Someone knocked on his door. "Come in."

The door opened, and Audrey's head appeared. "Did I hear you playing music from my phone on your video?"

"I'm sorry, I just . . ."

"Good choice. Your music is terrible."

She closed the door behind her. Micah smiled. He couldn't remember the last time she'd been so nice to him.

On Monday morning, as he headed to Miss Petunia's classroom to turn in the video, Micah had a strange, new sensation. He was feeling a lot of those lately. There was a little nervousness mixed in, but he mostly felt pride. Not the bad kind of pride, like Hanz always felt. No, Micah just felt confident that he was good at something and that he'd tried his best.

Just his luck, Hanz happened to be outside Miss Petunia's class when Micah got there.

"Vat are you doing?" Hanz asked. "How have you chosen to embarrass yourself today?"

"I'm just turning in the video for the talent show."

"Too bad ze video vas left up to you. I vanted to vatch my amazing performance again and again, but I'm sure it's trash now."

"Just your act." Micah knew he shouldn't have said it but couldn't help himself. He walked inside Miss Petunia's classroom before Hanz could respond.

The first people Micah saw in the room were PB and J. Why was the morning turning into a parade of all his worst enemies?

They both rolled their eyes when they saw Micah. "Are you ready to turn in your amazing video?" PB asked.

Miss Petunia had a big grin on her face too, but hers was genuine. She never suspected any mischief or meanness in her students, and her sarcasm detector was set at zero. "We can't wait to see what you've done! We're even going to grab a few clips for *The PB and J Report*!"

"If there's anything worth grabbing," J muttered under her breath.

"I hope so," Micah said. He smiled on the outside but couldn't help feeling nervous. What if everyone thought it was horrible?

That afternoon was the final test on the alien story in reading class. It was only a single question long:

What do you think is the most important theme of the story? Explain your answer.

Micah thought and thought. It wasn't as easy to concentrate on a test about a book as it was to concentrate when he was making videos. Maybe that was one of the ways you figured out your talent—it was the thing you liked to focus on.

At last, he came up with an answer. The story was about how everyone is different and good at different things. And that just because some people get recognized for their abilities more than other people, that doesn't make them any more important. Everybody matters.

Almost as soon as he finished writing, a voice came over the intercom. "Micah Murphy, please come to the principal's office."

Did he hear that right? He'd never been called down to the principal's office before.

"Ha! Glad it wasn't me this time!" Chet laughed. "Drury said next time I got busted he'd make me clean out the raccoon nests in the air-conditioning vents."

The Last Five Things Chet Claimed Mr. Drury Made Him Do

1. Stand on a rickety ladder and pull pencils out of the ceiling.

2. Watch Dennis eat his lunch: usually pastrami and mutton with a slice of Limburger cheese. On rye.

3. De-slug the front garden and feed the slugs to Mr. Harper's iguana. (Chet said this one was actually fun.)

4. Clean bird droppings off the scoreboard with old socks left in gym lockers.

5. Eat the cafeteria's turnip hash.

Micah headed out of the classroom. He figured he might as well just get it over with. Besides, there was no way Mr. Drury gave out crazy punishments like that. Or did he? No, he couldn't. But maybe . . .

His mind went back and forth all the way down the hall to the principal's office. It took him a long time to get there, mostly because he'd lost all feeling in his legs. At last, he arrived and stared at Mr. Drury's gold nameplate on the door. The door was a thick wooden monstrosity like it belonged in a castle. Particularly the dungeon part of the castle.

He knocked loudly. He'd meant to knock quietly, but it turned out he'd lost feeling in his arms too.

"Come in, Micah," Mr. Drury said. "Have a seat. Thanks for coming down."

As if I had a choice, Micah thought to himself.

Mr. Drury didn't wait for Micah to respond. "I wanted to talk to you about something."

Micah held his breath, wondering what was coming next.

"I heard you were the guy behind the video for the talent show. Miss Petunia told me she asked you to do it when she learned you wanted to get out of performing an act of your own. I just had a chance to watch the whole thing, beginning to end."

He paused, looking Micah in the eye, then said, "And I loved it."

Micah breathed out so hard he thought his chair might slide backward a little. "Thank you, sir."

"In fact, I was wondering if you'd be willing to film the band concert coming up next Tuesday. I could see this becoming a regular thing for you if you're not too busy."

It took Micah a while to realize Mr. Drury had stopped talking and was waiting for an answer. Then Micah forgot the question. Then he remembered the question but forgot how to talk. Finally, he pulled it together.

"Um. Er . . . I . . . Absolutely . . . I mean, yes! That sounds great! I'd love to, sir!"

And he meant every word of it.

Could It Be . . . ?

I cannot believe that Mr. Drury loved my video of the talent show so much he asked me to film the band concert. Is this my thing now?! Maybe it won't win me an Ultra Game-A-Tron 64, but honestly, I don't mind. Making videos is almost as awesome as playing *Captain Karate Dino Cop* . . . maybe better!

I have to admit, there were times throughout this whole process that I wondered what God was thinking when He made me. But I've learned I can trust Him and the plans He has for me.

You saw me before I was born. Every day of my life was recorded in your book.
Psalm 139:16 (NLT)

▷ **Why do YOU think it was important for Micah to trust God's plan?**

▷ **What is one special thing about YOU that comes from God?**

CHAPTER TWELVE

Friday was a good day. At lunch, Micah could actually read the inspirational posters on the wall without feeling like they were mocking him.

Armin put his lunch tray next to Micah's and sat down. "Everyone must've gone straight home yesterday and watched their copy of the video. It's all everybody's talking about today."

Lydia was sitting on Micah's other side. She smiled. "That must feel great, Micah!"

"Yeah. Actually, it does."

It was bean and mystery meat burrito day in the cafeteria, and Mr. Turtell was patrolling the room, keeping an eye out for contraband salsa. "Oh, hello, Micah," he said. "I watched the talent show video last night and didn't see you in it. I guess you never found your talent."

"No, but actually—"

"That Frank Millwood sure is something, though! He can unicycle and juggle and eat a taco and play football and swim and catch fish and . . ."

As Mr. Turtell walked away from the table, Lydia whispered to Micah, "At least he'll keep you humble!"

They could still hear him, two tables away. ". . . and play the fiddle and bake a soufflé and drive a forklift and knit an infinity scarf and . . ."

After lunch, they went out to the playground. The sky was blue, and the birds were chirping. Micah didn't mind at all.

"What should we do today?" Armin asked.

This was always a tough decision for Micah and his friends. There were so many options, and some of them were actually fun!

169

ACCORDING TO THE LATEST RESEARCH FROM *RECESS WEEKLY*,

The Top 6 Most Popular Playground Activities Among Fifth Graders at My School

6. Trying to "accidentally" kick balls onto the school roof so Dennis has to use the rickety ladder to get them down.

5. Counting how many wood chips you can sneak into Eddy Chilton's hoodie without him noticing.

4. Rolling down the hill, bowling for kindergartners.

3. Watching Ralph DeMill hide in the ball bin and scream when someone reaching for a kickball accidentally grabs his head.

2. In wide-eyed wonder, watching whatever Frank Millwood is doing like he's a famous athlete.

1. Dazed and confused, watching whatever Gabe is doing like he's a creature from another planet.

"Hey, Micah! How you doing?"

Micah turned around to see PB.

"Are you talking to me?" Micah asked.

"Of course we are!" J said. "Since you made that video, you're the coolest kid in fifth grade!"

"Yeah!" PB said. "We love you!"

"And we always will!" J added. "As long as you stay cool!"

"That sounds about right," Lydia mumbled under her breath.

Will Alameda, who'd been standing just behind PB and J, walked over to Micah. "I shouldn't have messed with your camera. I'm sorry about that."

"It's okay," said Micah. "I feel awful about accidentally making you sprain your wrists."

"It wasn't really your fault. I was just upset."

"Thanks. That makes me feel better."

"By the way, you didn't do a terrible job on the talent show video." Will smiled as he walked away.

Hanz walked up, fixing his hair in the reflection of his cell phone. "I zought ze video vas terrible. My dog Pouncer could've done a better job zan you. Everyone knows I vas ze star of ze show, but I vas only in ze video for five minutes!"

"But your act was only five minutes long," Micah said.

"A real director vould never make such an excuse!"

Micah didn't know what to say, so he turned to Armin and Lydia. "How about four square?"

"That sounds good," Armin said.

Lydia nodded. "Works for me."

"What a scoop!" J said. "Micah and friends play four square!"

PB nodded. "That'll be the lead story in our afternoon broadcast!"

When PB and J walked away, Armin and Lydia went to look for Gabe, so they'd have a fourth player. Micah went to the bin to grab a ball.

"Ahhhhh!" Ralph DeMill screamed at him from inside the bin.

"Ahhhhh!" screamed Micah.

He grabbed a ball and walked back over to Lydia and Armin. "Why do I always forget about that?"

Lydia nodded. "You are a remarkably easy target."

They played through the rest of recess. Just as the bell rang for them to line up to go back inside, Armin spiked the ball as hard as he could. Micah leaped up and barely tipped it with a finger as it passed over his head.

From out of nowhere, Frank Millwood dove behind him and caught the ball.

"Hey, Micah," he said, as he handed the ball over.

"Hey, Frank."

"Great job on that talent show video. It was

awesome!" Frank ran to catch up with his friends, and they all lined up to go inside.

Micah stood beside Armin, Lydia, and Gabe.

"Did you hear that?" Armin asked. "Mr. Perfect Millwood just said you did a great job! I guess you found your talent."

"Yeah." Lydia nodded. "We're proud of you, Micah."

Micah smiled. "Don't worry. It won't go to my head."

"How could it with Hanz around?" Armin said.

"And Chet," Lydia added.

"Don't forget Mr. Turtell," Armin said.

Micah shook his head. "I don't need them to keep me humble. I still don't know how to yo-yo!"

"I'll teach you!" Gabe pulled his yo-yo out of his pocket and started spinning it up and down. Then, to Micah's surprise, he stepped out of line and started doing his whole routine for the talent show. Around it went, faster and faster, twisting around his body and then uncoiling itself back into his hand. He had done the whole thing without a mistake!

"Wow!" Lydia said.

Micah nodded. "Way to go, Gabe!"

Grinning ear to ear, Gabe took a deep bow, going all the way down on one knee. As he bent forward, the yo-yo slipped out of his pocket and onto the ground. Quickly, he stood back up.

He should have looked where he was stepping. His left foot landed right on top of the yo-yo, and it slipped out from under him, knocking him on his back. Meanwhile, his foot accidentally flipped the yo-yo up in the air, launching it high in the sky over his body, until at last, it landed—*plunk!*—right on his forehead.

Micah stared at him with a smile. "Yeah, that seems about right."

Created on Purpose

What a week! If you had told me it would all turn out this way, I wouldn't have believed you. I think it may be months before I stop having nightmares about being onstage next to Miss Petunia, in a squash costume. I managed to avoid the stage altogether because I found my place behind the camera . . . and that's exactly where I was meant to be.

I don't know if you've ever been through this type of thing . . . searching and trying and failing over and over again to find your "thing." I'm sure we all go through this at some point in our lives. I can't say I enjoyed the journey, but I did learn a few things in the process.

GOOD FRIENDS ARE CRUCIAL TO SURVIVING LIFE

More important than a fierce kick is to Captain Karate Dino Cop or the library is to Lydia's existence, the right friends will carry you through life's toughest moments. If you don't have good people in your life, stop everything and go find them . . . like, now! (Well, finish the book first. You're almost there!)

GOD DOESN'T MAKE MISTAKES

He created us on purpose. He knew what He was doing when He made our incredibly awesome world and when He made YOU and me. You can trust Him through the process. He won't let you down.

I guess we've answered the question on whether or not I've got talent. It seems like I do. It may not look like everyone else's, and it may not win me a talent show, but my talent is special because it's mine and I know that as I follow God, He'll show me how to use it to help others and have fun.

Each of you should use whatever gift you have received to serve others, as faithful stewards of God's grace in its various forms. If anyone speaks, they should do so as one who speaks the very words of God. If anyone serves, they should do so with the strength God provides, so that in all things God may be praised through Jesus Christ.
1 Peter 4:10–11 (NIV)

▷ **What did YOU learn through Micah's journey of discovering his God-given gift?**

▷ **Why do YOU think God made each of us unique?**

MR. DRURY

PRINCIPAL

MRS. GRITTNER

ENGLISH

MEET THE

MR. PETUNIA

DRAMA

MR. TURTELL
HISTORY

MR. BEAKER
SCIENCE

TEACHERS

MR. SPINOZA
ART

DENNIS
CUSTODIAL ARTS

About the Author

Andy McGuire has written and illustrated four children's books, including *Remy the Rhino* and *Rainy Day Games*. He has a BA in creative writing from Miami University and an MA in literature from Ohio University. Andy's writing heroes have always been the ones who make him laugh, from Roald Dahl and Louis Sachar to P. G. Wodehouse and William Goldman. Andy lives with his wife and three children in Burnsville, Minnesota.

About the Illustrator

Girish Manuel is the creator of the Micah's Super Vlog video series and a producer at Square One World Media. He lives in a little place called Winnipeg, Canada, with his lovely wife, Nikki, and furry cat, Paska. Girish enjoys running and drawing . . . but not at the same time. That would be hard. He tried it once and got ink all over his shoes.

Have you ever felt bad for something you did?
We all do stuff that we shouldn't do.
Maybe we've told a lie, or even stolen something . . .
When we go our own way instead of God's, it's called **SIN**.
Sin keeps us from being close to God
and it has some other serious consequences . . .

but I've got some good news!

GOD LOVES YOU!!

°Yes, the amazing,
incredible,
Creator who made the universe
and everything in it
(including YOU)
loves you!

How do I know this?

Because God is my friend. And He wants to be your friend too!

Check this out:

When we sin, the payment is death (Romans 6:23). But God gives us the gift of eternal life (John 3:16). That's because of what Jesus did for us on the cross.

What did Jesus do exactly?

Jesus, God's very own son, came down to earth to save us from our sin and restore our relationship with God! He did that by living a perfect life (without sin!) and taking the punishment for OUR sins when He was nailed to a cross (a punishment for really bad criminals back then)!

Jesus did this because He loved us enough to take OUR punishment! But that's not the end of the story. Three days after His death, Jesus rose from the grave, proving that God has power over sin and death!

So, what now?

Even though there's countless things we have done wrong, God can forgive our sins ... no matter how many or how big they are! He wants to have a relationship with you through Jesus!

Check this out:

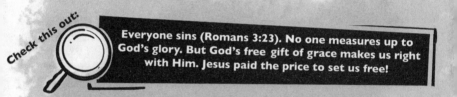

Everyone sins (Romans 3:23). No one measures up to God's glory. But God's free gift of grace makes us right with Him. Jesus paid the price to set us free!

How?

Even though we can't do anything to save ourselves from sin, we can be saved because of what Jesus has already done! By trusting Him with your life, you can live free from guilt and shame, knowing that YOU ARE LOVED!

If you're ready to accept God's gift and live LOVED, simply pray this prayer:

Dear Jesus, thank You for loving me and dying on the cross for my sins. Today I accept God's gift of salvation and I invite You to be the King of my heart. Please forgive me of my sins and guide me as I grow in friendship with You. Jesus, I want to be more like You and share Your love with others. Thank You that I don't have to be perfect but can grow in faith as I follow Your ways. In Your name I pray, amen.

CAPTAIN KARATE DINO COP IN:
OVERDUE JUSTICE!

I'm on the lookout for something bad. Something ugly. Something that will keep you up at night...

OVERDUE LIBRARY BOOKS.

Reports show the missing books were the same topics...karate, dinosaurs, and law enforcement.

Something tells me this is **PERSONAL**.

STEP!

All evidence leads to this warehouse!

WORD SEARCH!

```
D S R L T M N Z X W S A R S I L A B N
E X T R A V A G A N Z A U A P M E V B
L T S V C R R X Z S R P Q R E D E I D
Q A B T A L E N T V K R M W R L O D E
S Y I L X P B C A Z S C E Q F L S E H
X C N M S D E P E Y W B T E O P Q O S
P K T C A Z Q Y N S Z T A Y R O L G K
E L E P D B S A J A S I P W M I C A L
B V R A S E U H U D E M H S A S A M I
D T M S R S P R G O Y R O I N T H E P
Y J I I A E D S G R H N R J C R D W H
O B S R L U E A L S I D Y S E I P N A
Y A S E X P M Q I I Z I P C I N W S I
O E I Z A R G O N O I T N M R B I Y K
I L O P Q X A L G U E U P M D E T Y E
N L N K S Z O Q S D O D G E B A L L W
G Z X K T A L I L P Z M N S H E D U L
```

Talent
Juggling
YoYoing
Recess
Video Game
Pouncer
Metaphor
Dodgeball
Zargon
Intermission
Performance
Extravaganza

CHECK OUT ↴
www. MicahsSuperVlog.com